PRAISE FOR
GIORGIO SCERBANENCO

"A gem ... A vivid portrait of Milan's seamy underbelly ... Scerbanenco reveals Duca Lamberti to us; in doing so, he also unveils the Italian hardboiled hero." **—CRIME FICTION LOVER**

"Scerbanenco's dark, moody novels have much in common with the darkest of Scandinavian crime fiction ... This forgotten noir classic from 1966 is finally available in translation. That's good news!" **—LIBRARY JOURNAL**

"There is courage in his books, the courage to call things by their name ... No filters shield you from the reality, which is as desperate, fierce, and stark as in the best novels of James Ellroy or Jim Thompson." **—CARLO LUCARELLI**

"[Scerbanenco can be] as dark as Leonardo Sciascia, as deadpan realistic as Maj Sjöwall and Per Wahlöö, as probing in his observation of people as incisive as humane as Camilleri, as noir as Manchette, but with a dark, dark humor all his own." **—DETECTIVES BEYOND BORDERS**

"The Duca Lamberti novels are world-class noir, and their publication in English is long, long overdue." **—THE COMPLETE REVIEW**

GIORGIO SCERBANENCO was born in Kiev in 1911 to a Ukrainian father and an Italian mother, grew up in Rome, and moved to Milan at the age of eighteen. In the 1930s, he worked as a journalist and attempted some early forays into fiction. In 1943, as German forces advanced on the city, Scerbanenco escaped over the Alps to Switzerland, carrying nothing but a hundred pages of a new novel he was working on. He returned to Milan in 1945 and resumed his prolific career, writing for women's magazines, including a very popular advice-for-the-lovelorn column, and publishing dozens of novels and short stories. But he is best known for the four books he wrote at the end of his life that make up the Milano Quartet, *A Private Venus*, *Traitors to All*, *The Boys of the Massacre*, and *The Milanese Kill on Saturdays*. Scerbanenco drew on his experiences as an orderly for the Milan Red Cross in the 1930s to create his protagonist Duca Lamberti, a disbarred doctor; it was during this period that he came to know another, more desperate side of his adopted city. The quartet of novels was immediately hailed as noir classics, and on its publication in 1966, *Traitors to All* received the most prestigious European crime prize, the Grand Prix de Littérature Policière. The annual prize for the best Italian crime novel, the Premio Scerbanenco, is named after him. He died in 1969 in Milan.

HOWARD CURTIS translates books from French, Italian, and Spanish, and was awarded the John Florio Prize (2004) as well as the Europa Campiello Literary Prize (2010).

A PRIVATE VENUS

A PRIVATE VENUS

GIORGIO SCERBANENCO

TRANSLATED BY HOWARD CURTIS

MELVILLE HOUSE
BROOKLYN · LONDON

MELVILLE
INTERNATIONAL
CRIME

MELVILLE INTERNATIONAL CRIME

A PRIVATE VENUS

First published in Italy in 1966 as *Venere Privata* by
Edizioni Garzanti S.p.A., Milano
Copyright © 1966 Giorgio Scerbanenco Estate
Published in agreement with Agenzia Letteraria Internazionale
First published in the United Kingdom by Hersilia Press
Translation copyright © 2012 Hersilia Press

First Melville House printing: March 2014

Melville House Publishing   8 Blackstock Mews
145 Plymouth Street   and   Islington
Brooklyn, NY 11201   London N4 2BT

mhpbooks.com   facebook.com/mhpbooks   @melvillehouse

ISBN: 978-1-61219-335-9

Manufactured in the United States of America
1 3 5 7 9 10 8 6 4 2

A catalog record for this book is
available from the Library of Congress.

A PRIVATE VENUS

PROLOGUE FOR A SHOP ASSISTANT

'What's your name?'

'Antonio Marangoni. I live over there in Cascina Luasca; I've been going to Rogoredo by bicycle every morning for more than fifty years.'

'Don't waste your time on these old geezers, let's go back to the paper.'

'He's the one who found the girl, he can describe her for us, otherwise we'll have to go to the morgue, and we're already late.'

'I saw her when the ambulance arrived, she was wearing a sky-blue dress.'

'A sky-blue dress. What colour hair?'

'Dark, but not black.'

'Dark, but not black.'

'She had these big round sunglasses.'

'Round sunglasses.'

'I couldn't see much of her face, it was covered by her hair.'

'Move on please, there's nothing to see.'

'There's nothing to see, the officer's right, let's go back to the paper.'

'Move on, now. Why aren't you lot at school?'

'Yes, what are all these kids doing here?'

'When I arrived I could smell blood.'

'Go on, Signor Marangoni.'

'I could smell blood.'

'Yes, she must have lost a lot of blood.'

'I couldn't smell anything, too much time had passed before we got here in the van.'

'Go on, officer.'

'They'll tell you all you need to know at Headquarters. I'm here to keep the riff-raff away, I don't talk to reporters. But you couldn't smell the blood, that's just not possible.'

'Well, *I* smelt it, and I have a good nose. I got off my bike because I needed to pass water, I put the bike down on the ground.'

'Go on, Signor Marangoni.'

'I went to the bushes, the ones over there, and that's when I saw the foot, well the shoe anyway.'

'Move on now, keep moving, there's nothing to see, all these people looking at a bit of empty field.'

'At first all I saw was the shoe, I didn't see the foot inside it, so I reached out my hand.'

'Alberta Radelli, twenty-three years old, shop assistant, found in Metanopoli, near Cascina Luasca, the body was found at 5:30 in the morning by Signor Antonio Marangoni, sky-blue dress, dark hair, not black, round glasses, I'll go and phone this in, then I'll come back and pick you up.'

'Then I realised there was a foot inside the shoe and I felt sick, I moved all those weeds and I saw her, it was obvious straight away that she was dead.'

PART ONE

Isn't summing up a man's life a kind of prayer?

1

After three years in prison he had learned to pass the time with whatever was at hand, but for the first ten minutes he smoked a cigarette without thinking of any game to play. It was only when he threw the cigarette end down on the gravel drive that it struck him: the number of little stones in the various drives and garden paths was a finite number. Even the number of grains of sand in all the beaches in the world was a finite number that could be calculated, however large it was, and so, staring down at the ground, he started to count. In five square centimetres there might be an average of eighty stones, so he calculated visually the area of all the drives and paths that led to the villa ahead of him and concluded that all the gravel in all the drives, which seemed infinite, consisted of a mere one million six hundred thousand stones, with a ten per cent margin of error.

Then, suddenly, there was a crunching sound on the gravel, and he lifted his head for a moment: a man had emerged from the villa and was coming along the biggest drive towards him. Now that the man had appeared he had time to play a game, so, sitting on that small concrete shelf that functioned as a bench, he leaned forward and picked up a handful of stones. The game consisted of guessing two things: one, if the number of stones was an odd or even number, and two, if that number was higher or lower than a chosen number: twenty, for example. To win you had to guess both things. He estimated that he had an even number of stones in his fist, and a number lower than twenty. He opened his fist and counted: he had won, there were eighteen stones.

'I'm so sorry to have kept you waiting, Dr. Lamberti.' The man had come level with him, and his voice was solemn and tired, the voice of a weary emperor. Leaning forward like that, Duca saw only the man's legs, thin legs inside narrow trousers: a young man's trousers, although the man wasn't young, as he saw as soon as he got up to shake the hand he was holding out. He was a middle-aged man, little but powerful, his hair shaved to almost nothing, his beard shaved down to the root, his hand also little but with a grip of steel.

'Good evening,' he said to the little emperor. 'Pleased to meet you.' In prison he had learned not to say more than he needed to. At his trial, while Signora Maldrigati's niece was crying over her murdered aunt, but omitting to mention the millions she had inherited from that same aunt, he had wanted to speak, but his defence lawyer, almost with tears in his eyes, had whispered in his ear that he shouldn't say a word, not one: he would tell the truth, and the truth is death; anything but the truth in a courtroom, at a trial. Or in life.

'It's very hot in Milan,' the little man said, and sat down next to him on the concrete bench. 'Here in the Brianza, on the other hand, it's always cool. Do you know the Brianza?'

He couldn't have called him here to talk about the weather in the Brianza, he was just building up to it. 'Yes,' he replied, 'as a boy I used to come here by bicycle, Canzo, Asso, the lake.'

'By bicycle,' the little man said. 'I used to come here by bicycle, too, when I was young.'

The conversation seemed to be over. In the dusk, the garden was almost dark, some lights went on in the villa, a bus passed on the main road twenty metres below the villa, its horn sounding almost like a piece by Wagner.

'It's gone out of fashion these days,' the little man resumed, 'they all chase the sun on the French Riviera or the islands, whereas here in the Brianza, only half an hour's drive from Milan, the air's as clear as if you were in Tahiti. I think it's because people always want to go a long way from where they are. A place is never beautiful if it's too close. My son regards this villa as a kind of punishment cell, whenever I tell him to come here he does it as a penance. Maybe he's right: it may be cooler, but it's a bit boring.' It was almost dark now, the lighted windows in the villa were the only light. In a different voice, the little man said, 'Were you told why I wanted to see you, Dr. Lamberti?'

No, Duca said, he hadn't been told. What he had been told, though, was who this man who seemed so modest, so simple, really was: one of the magnificent five, in other words one of the top five engineers in the field of plastics, Engineer Pietro Auseri, late fifties, a man who could create anything out of anything; a special kind of plastic was named after him, Auserolo, he had three degrees, his fortune must be considerable, but officially he was only a freelance engineer with an old office in an old street in Milan.

'I thought they would have told you,' the little man said. The tiredness had gone from his voice, only the authority remained, he had clearly said all he had to say on the topics of the weather and tourism.

'All I was told was that you might have a job for me,' Duca said. It was dark now, more lights came on in the villa, a dim trail of light reached as far as the spot where they were.

'Yes, in a way it's a job,' Auseri said. 'Do you mind if we talk here? My son's in the house and I don't want you to see him until after we've talked.'

'That's fine by me.' He liked this little middle-aged man: he was no fool. Over the past few years, inside prison and out, Duca had seen whole armies of fools and he could almost tell them from the smell, from a finger, from a single hair in their eyebrows.

'You're a doctor,' Auseri said.

He didn't reply immediately, but a few moments later, and in that darkness, in that silence, it was a long pause. 'I was. I'm sure you were told.'

'Certainly,' Auseri said, 'but you're still a doctor. And I need a doctor.'

Duca counted the windows in the villa: there were eight of them, four on the ground floor and four on the first floor. 'I can't practice any more. I can't even give injections—especially not injections. Weren't you told?'

'I was told everything, but it doesn't matter.'

Curious. 'If you need a doctor,' Duca said, 'and choose

one who's been struck off the register and can't even prescribe an aspirin, then it must matter a bit.'

'No,' the emperor said, politely but authoritatively. In the darkness he held out the packet of cigarettes. 'Do you smoke?'

'I even spent three years in prison.' He took a cigarette and Auseri lit it for him. 'For murder.'

'I know,' Auseri said, 'but it doesn't matter.'

Then maybe nothing really mattered.

'My son is an alcoholic,' Auseri said in the darkness, smoking. 'He's in that room on the first floor right now, the only lighted window on the first floor. That's his room. He must have managed to hide a few bottles of whisky from me, and he's tanking himself up while he's waiting for us.'

From his voice, it was obvious that his son didn't matter all that much to him either.

'He's twenty-two,' Auseri said, 'two metres tall and weighs, I think, ninety kilos. Up until last year he didn't worry me too much, the only thing that made me a bit sad was that he wasn't very bright. I couldn't send him to university, I only managed to get him through his high school exams by bribing his teachers. He's also very shy and submissive. To be honest, he's a big lump.'

In other words, tall and stupid. Auseri's bitter voice seemed to come from out of nowhere, it somehow just materialised in the dark air.

'I wasn't too upset that he was like that,' Auseri said. 'I don't care about the joy having a genius as a son may bring. When he was nineteen, I sent him to work for Montecatini.

He went through all the offices and departments, so that he could learn; he didn't learn much, but he kept going. Then last year he started drinking. For the first few months he managed to hide his vice, then he started going in late to work, or not going in at all, then I had to keep him at home because he was going into work with whisky bottles, the flat kind, in his pocket. You are listening, aren't you?'

Oh, yes, in prison he had learned to listen; his cellmates all had long stories to tell, lies of course, stories about how they were innocent, how they'd been ruined by women, every one of them was an Abel killed by Cain or an Adam corrupted by Eve. The engineer, though, was telling him something different, something sadder and more meaningful, and he was really listening. 'Of course,' he replied.

'I need to explain a lot of things so that you'll understand,' Auseri said. In the darkness, his voice did not lose any of its authority, but rather became more stubborn. 'My son gets drunk three times a day. By lunchtime he's completely drunk, he doesn't eat anything and falls asleep. In the afternoon he gets drunk a second time, then sleeps until dinnertime. At dinner he eats, but he begins with the third course, and falls asleep in his chair. That's what he's been doing for most of the past year, unless I've physically prevented him.'

For a twenty-two-year-old it was a worrying way of drinking. 'You must have tried a lot of things to stop him from drinking.' He couldn't yet figure out what was wanted of him, but he was making an effort to be polite. 'Keeping him away from whichever friends of his are making him drink.'

'My son doesn't have any friends,' Auseri said. 'He's never

had any, not even in elementary school. He's an only child. I was widowed eleven years ago but, busy as I've been with my work, I never abandoned him to tutors and governesses. I know him well, he's never played tennis with anyone, he's never gone to the swimming pool, to the gym, or to a dance with friends. Since he's had his car, he's only used it for drives along the autostrada. The only normal thing about him is that he likes driving fast. One of these days he'll kill himself, and his alcohol problem will be solved.'

Duca waited for the bitter emperor to start speaking again. He had to wait a long time.

'I did a lot of things to stop him drinking.' Auseri was in expository mode now, as if listing the sections of a disastrous balance sheet. 'The first method was persuasion, talking to him. I've never in my life known anybody to be persuaded of anything with words, but I had to try. Psychologists say young people need to be persuaded, not controlled, but my attempts at persuasion were all defeated by the whisky. I talked, and he drank. Then I tried the restrictive method. No money, maximum surveillance, I was with him for almost two weeks, without ever leaving him alone. We were in St. Moritz; we passed the hours looking at the swans on the lake, with our umbrellas in our hands, because it rained all the time, but he managed to drink all the same, he drank at night, because we slept in separate rooms. Somebody working in the hotel must have brought him something to drink without my knowledge, and by the morning he was blind drunk.'

Every now and again they looked at the only lighted

window on the first floor: the drinker's room, though all you could see was the light, the play of light on the ceiling.

'The third method didn't give any better results,' Auseri said. 'I'm a great believer in corporal punishment. Slaps and punches force a man to think fast about the best way to avoid them. Every time I found my son drunk, I'd hit him, a lot, and hard. My son respects me, and even if he'd tried to rebel I would have crushed him. After that corporal punishment, my son would cry and try to tell me that it wasn't his fault, that he didn't want to drink, but couldn't stop himself. After a while, I abandoned that method, too.'

'Have you tried any others?'

'No. I did call a doctor and talk to him about the matter, and he told me that the only way was to put my son in a detox clinic.'

Yes, it was true, in a clinic they would detoxify the young man and then as soon as he got out he would probably start drinking again. But he didn't say this: Auseri did.

'I'd already thought of putting him in a clinic, but when he comes out he'll only start drinking again: as soon as he's alone he starts drinking. He needs friends, he needs women.' Auseri offered him another cigarette and lit it and they started smoking. The air was still damp, and now it was also dark, apart from the lighted windows at the end of the drive. 'Especially women. I've never known him to have a girlfriend. Don't get me wrong. He likes women, I can tell that from the way he looks at them, and I believe he often uses prostitutes. But he's too introverted to get a girlfriend. I've seen girls run after him, he's a good match after all, but he clams up when he's with a woman, he literally never opens his mouth. He may give the impression of not being normal. But that's wrong. He did the whole of his military service, and as a private, not an officer. At first his companions teased him, because he always kept himself to himself. He almost broke one fellow's head and cracked another's ribs, after that they respected him and left him alone. My son is normal, he just takes after his mother. She was like that, too, she had no friends, or even acquaintances, she was quite happy to stay at home with me. I only ever managed to take her to receptions or parties a few times. Defects can be inherited, whereas qualities are recessive. It's a kind of biological entropy.'

The little emperor waved a hand, unhappily, but in the darkness it almost didn't seem like a living hand, it appeared as vague and phosphorescent as ectoplasm, and even more unhappy in that funereal darkness.

'And now I'd like to make one last attempt,' Auseri said, 'put him together with someone who could be both a friend and a doctor, who'd use any method he wanted to, to make him stop drinking, who'd stop him physically every minute of the day, even in the toilet. I don't care if it takes a year, or what means he uses, he could even beat him to death, I'd rather he was dead than an alcoholic.'

In prison you can actually become intelligent, and words mean a lot, the words you say and those you listen to. Outside, where you were free to say what you liked, words, and listening to words, were wasted, underestimated: people spoke without knowing what they were saying, and listened without understanding. But with Auseri it wasn't like that. That was why Duca liked him, apart from the pain and bitterness concealed within the imperious exterior. He said, 'You want me to be that person who's both a friend and a doctor, and who gets him off the drink.'

'Yes, the idea came to me yesterday. Superintendent Carrua is a friend of mine, he knows the whole story. I had to go to Police Headquarters yesterday and I dropped by his office. He talked to me about you, and asked me if I could find you a job with Montecatini. Of course I could find you a desk job with Montecatini if you wanted it, but then it struck me that someone like you could help me with my son.'

Of course, someone who's only been out of prison for three days helps everyone, does everything, sings any song. He was certainly lucky to be a friend of Superintendent Carrua's, he already had many things to choose from. Carrua had also found him a job selling pharmaceuticals, it was the ideal profession for a doctor who had been struck off, a suitcase with samples, a car with *Ciba* or *Farmitalia* painted on the doors, driving around the region, calling on doctors and pharmacists: it was almost better than being a doctor yourself. Or if he preferred something more unusual, he could accept Engineer Auseri's offer and devote himself to his alcoholic son, cure him, remove the poison from him, be a kind of social worker. Or if he had lost the taste for socially redeeming work, he could make sure that Auseri got him that position with Montecatini: a desk somewhere in one of those neat offices, he could gratify his small-minded selfishness, the inertia of a man who no longer believes in anything. But in prison you also become sensitive, easily irritated. And because he was irritated now, he said calmly, 'What made you think of me? Any other doctor could treat your son.'

'I don't think so,' Auseri said. He had become irritated, too. 'I need a person I can trust absolutely. From the way Superintendent Carrua spoke to me about you, I know I can trust you. I have an intuition about these things. Earlier, when I saw you sitting here, with those stones in your hand, I knew I could trust you.'

These weren't empty words, he could hear it in the tone of Auseri's voice, and his irritation vanished. He liked talking to a man, after having talked to so many fools: the director of the clinic in the beanie hat who told dirty jokes as he operated, the prosecuting lawyer who shook his head each time he uttered Duca's name in his closing statement: '. . . I don't understand how Dr. Duca Lamberti'—a shake of the head—'can maintain such an absurd version of events. Dr. Duca Lamberti'—a shake of the head—'is either more na- ive, or more cunning, than may appear. Dr. Duca Lam- berti'—another shake of the head—how could anyone be such an idiot? Auseri, though, was a man, and he liked lis- tening to him.

'Any other doctor would take advantage of the situation to drum up publicity for himself,' Auseri said. 'Until now my son's alcoholism has been a closely guarded secret, known only to a few discreet friends. With any other doctor, it would become an item of gossip in all the drawing rooms in Milan. But you won't talk, and I know that if you accept the job you'll get it done. Another doctor would get bored after a week and leave the boy stuffed full of pills and injections, and he'll get drunk anyway. I don't want pills and injections. I want a friend and an inflexible guardian for my son. It's my final attempt. If it doesn't work, I'll let him go, I'll cut him off and wash my hands of him.'

Now it was his turn. What time was it, and where were they? In a damp dark corner of the Brianza, on the side of a hill, with a villa ahead that seemed to be sliding towards them and inside the villa a young man clinging to a bottle of whisky, that was where they were. 'I need to ask you a few questions,' he said.

'Of course,' Auseri said.

'You say your son has been drinking like this for a year. Did he drink before? Or did he just suddenly start drinking?'

'No, he drank before as well, but not very often, he'd get drunk two or three times a month, no more than that. I don't want to be ungenerous towards his dead mother, but it's a tendency he gets from her.'

'You also told me your son has no friends, no girlfriends. Does that mean he usually drinks alone?'

'He's drinking alone right now, in his room. But he drinks alone because he's never with anybody. He doesn't want to be.'

'You also said that, despite appearances, your son is a normal young man. I'm prepared to believe that. But a normal young man doesn't start drinking in that way without a reason. Something may have happened to him that drove him to drink more than he did before. He may have got involved with a woman, for example. In films, men drink to forget unhappy love affairs.'

Auseri's hand rose again, floated in the dark air, and moved across his face. 'That was what I asked him when I hit him with the poker. We have a fireplace in our apartment in Milan, an old-fashioned one with a poker. A poker on the face hurts, and as it happened quite recently you can still see the mark on his cheek. I asked him if there was a woman, if he was in debt because he'd had to pay for some under-age girl to have an abortion, he said no, and I believe him, because he's useless—even at doing something wrong.'

He must be a strange young man. 'I'm sorry to insist, Engineer, I'm speaking now as a doctor,' as an ex-doctor, of course, a doctor who's been struck off, 'you told me before that as far as women are concerned, your son doesn't have girlfriends, he's always turned to prostitutes. Given this habit, it's possible he's contracted what he thinks of as a terrible disease and in his desperation, considering him-self human refuse, has started drinking. Syphilis is a less fearsome disease now than it was in the past, but it's still a stigma, and a sensitive young man like your son could well find it traumatic.'

In the darkness, Auseri said, 'That was the first thing I suspected, and four months ago I had him see a doctor. He was given all kinds of tests. He's in perfect health, no infec-tion at all, not even the most commonplace.'

So not even the fear of disease was driving young Auseri to drink. 'But what does your son say? What excuse does he give?'

'My son is humiliated and desperate. He says he doesn't want to drink but can't help himself. Whenever I hit him, he says to me, "You're right, you're right," and starts crying.'

It was time for Duca to make up his mind. 'Have you told your son about me?'

'Certainly.' Auseri used that word often, which coming from him meant that he was absolutely sure, he wasn't wasting his breath. 'I told him that a doctor I really trust might agree to help him, and he promised me that he'll do whatever you want. Even if he hadn't promised, I'd have made him do it all the same.'

Naturally, or even: certainly. What should he do? This wasn't a job, it was shaping up to be a right old mess, but the idea of being a pharmaceuticals salesman, when he thought about it, did rather turn his stomach. He tried to be calm, not to become irritated with himself. 'I don't think it'll be difficult to stop your son from drinking. In little more than a month you can have him teetotal again. What will be difficult, if not impossible, is to stop him starting again, as soon as he's free. Alcoholism is a symptom here, if we don't find the cause, we'll be back at square one.'

'Start by making him teetotal, and then we'll see.'

'All right. I'm ready.' It was time to meet this victim of alcohol.

'Thank you.' But Auseri did not get up, he looked for something in his pockets. 'If it's all right with you, I want to leave him in your hands immediately and not have to deal with him again. I've been watching him for a month, and I'm exhausted. Seeing him drunk from morning to night is depressing. I've written this cheque for you, and there's some cash, too, to cover your first expenses. I'll hand my son over to you now, and then I'm going straight back to Milan, I have to be in Pavia by six o'clock tomorrow morning. I've already neglected my work long enough for him. Do whatever you want: you have carte blanche.'

In the darkness, he couldn't tell the cheque from the cash, it was just a little wad of papers of a certain thickness, and Duca put them in his pocket. Engineer Auseri was well aware that people who are just out of prison don't have very much to fall back on.

'Let's go.'

They started climbing towards the villa. When they entered, a young man stood up somewhat unsteadily from an armchair, but managed to stay on his feet without sway-ing. The living room of the villa was small, too small for him, it was like a doll's house with him inside, not a real villa.

'My son Davide. Dr. Duca Lamberti.'

2

It all happened very quickly: the little emperor with the narrow trousers had grown weary again, he came out with a few more lines, like an exhausted actor, his son would do the honours, he said, he was sorry he couldn't stay, he seemed reluctant to even look at his son, he said goodbye to him with his back turned, then held out his hand to say goodbye to Duca and said, 'Phone if you have to, but it won't be so easy to reach me for a while,' which was probably just a polite way of saying that he didn't want to be disturbed. 'Thank you very much, Dr. Lamberti,' and only as he was about to disappear into the garden did he look for a moment at the gigantic young man who was his son, and in that look there was a bit of everything, just like in a supermarket: compassion, hate, fierce love, irony, contempt, a painful fatherly affection.

Then the crunch of his steps on the gravel, then silence, then the muted roar of an engine, the dull sound of tyres on the drive, then nothing.

They stood for a while in silence, barely looking at each other. Davide Auseri swayed only twice in all that time, but elegantly: there was nothing vulgar about his drunkenness, especially as far as his face was concerned. What was the expression on that face? Duca tried to figure it out, and then realised: it was the face of a schoolboy at a major exam who can't answer a question: a mixture of anguish and shyness, and a few wretched attempts to appear natural.

It was a gentle face, a pageboy's face, and yet manly, as yet unravaged by the alcohol. Elegant, too, was the parting on one side of his dark blond hair, the stubble on his cheeks, the white shirt with the long sleeves rolled up on his big arms with their coating of down, the black cotton trousers, the opaque black shoes: the model of a respectable young Milanese, with an echo of British style, as if Milan was somehow, morally, part of the Commonwealth.

'Let's sit down,' Duca said to Davide, who swayed one last time, then eased himself into an armchair. He said it to him sternly, because even though he had been in prison he still had a heart, in the form not so much of a cardiac muscle, but like one of those hearts you still see drawn on greetings cards. Sternness masks your own emotion, your own weakness. Even a doctor can be upset by a moral disease, and this young man was morally ill. 'Who's in the villa apart from us?' he asked him, again sternly.

'In the villa, let's see,' the exam question wasn't difficult, not as difficult as the mere fact of speaking to a stranger must have been for the young man, 'in this villa, let's call it a house, well, there's the maid, who's the wife of the gardener, there's a butler, and then there's the cook, she's making dinner right now, even daddy says you can't really call her a cook, but these days you just have to make do . . .' He was smiling as he spoke, playing beautifully the part of a brilliant young conversationalist.

'Anyone else?' Duca cut in, harshly.

The giant young man's eyes clouded over with fear. 'Nobody,' he said immediately.

It was a difficult case. He mustn't make a mistake in establishing a rapport: the young man was drunk, but quite lucid. 'Try not to be afraid of me, or we won't get anywhere.'

'I'm not afraid,' Davide said, swallowing with fear.

'It's only natural for you to be afraid, you've never seen me before and you know you're going to have to do everything I say. It's not the most pleasant of situations, but it's what your father wanted. I'd like to start my work by speaking ill of your father, if you'll allow me.' The young man did not smile at all, a teacher's witticisms never makes the frightened examinee smile. 'Your father has crushed you, he's always imposed his will on you, he's stopped you becoming a man. I'm here to help you kick the drink habit, and I can do that easily, but it's not your real illness. You don't treat a son as if he was still a child who has to sit quietly at the table. Your father made that mistake and I can't remedy that, and won't even try. When you've got out of the habit of drinking, I'll leave you, and it'll be a relief for both of us. So you should try to be as little afraid as possible. Apart from anything else, it bothers me when people are afraid of me.'

'I'm not afraid, doctor.' He seemed more afraid than ever.

'Drop that. And drop the "doctor." I don't like being too familiar too soon, but in this case it's necessary. We'll call each other by our first names.' It would be a mistake trying to become his friend, to lure him in: the young man was intelligent, sensitive, he would never believe such a sudden friendship. Better the truth, even though he could still hear his defence lawyer whispering in his ear: never, never, never the truth, better death.

Then the elderly maid came in. She looked more like a peasant woman who had entered the villa by mistake and was disconcerted to see them there. She asked sourly if she should lay the table, and for how many. 'It's half past eight,' she added, almost with derision.

Even this question brought anxiety into the pageboy's sad eyes, and Duca had to resolve it. 'Let's eat out. Tell the staff they can have the evening off.'

'We're eating out,' Davide said to the sour woman, who looked at them mockingly for a moment then disappeared from the room as randomly as she had entered it.

But before taking the young man out, Duca decided he needed to give him a medical examination, and so he asked Davide to take him upstairs to his room, and there told him to undress. Davide stripped down to his pants but Duca gestured to him to take them off. He was even more impressive naked than clothed, and Duca felt as if he was in Florence, looking at Michelangelo's David, grown a little fat, but only a little.

'I know it's a bother, but turn around and walk.'

Davide obeyed like a child, worse, like a laboratory mouse following a pre-arranged path according to the impulses received, except that he couldn't turn with much precision and swayed more than before.

'That's enough. Now lie down on the bed.' Apart from these motor disorders due to his drunken state, his walk presented no abnormalities. When he was on the bed, Duca felt his liver, and for what such a rudimentary examination was worth, it could have been a teetotaller's liver. He looked at his tongue: perfect; he examined his skin centimetre by centimetre: perfect, although the texture was undoubtedly masculine, it was as limpid and elastic as that of a beautiful woman. Even alcohol would take time to eat away at this physical monument.

There might be some failure elsewhere. 'Stay there on the bed,' he said, 'just tell me where I can find a pair of scissors.'

'In the bathroom, just go out in the corridor, it's next door.'

He came back from the bathroom with the scissors and began pricking Davide's feet, his calves, his legs, with one or both of the points of the scissors. The answers were always clear: young Davide was a drinker on whom alcohol had so far had absolutely no effect.

'You can get dressed again, then we'll go to dinner. I think there's a place near Inverigo.' He looked out of the window while Davide dressed, then said, 'Your father may have told you I'm only just out of prison.' It wasn't a question.

'Yes.'

'Then I'm sure you'll understand. We'll start the treatment tomorrow. Tonight I'd like to relax. Quite apart from the surroundings, a prison diet is depressing. Tonight you'll be the one to keep me company.'

Before they went out, Duca made Davide stop under the light and passed two fingers over his left cheek, where there was what looked like a coal smudge, only it wasn't coal.

'Does it hurt?'

'Yes.' He seemed less afraid. 'Not much, only at night. It's best if I don't sleep on that side.'

'Hitting you with a poker was a bit extreme.'

For the first time Davide smiled. 'I'd drunk a bit too much that night.' He was excusing his father, he thought the punishment was just, he would have turned the other cheek for a second blow.

The strange young man's car was a Giulietta, dark blue obviously, and obviously with a grey interior, obviously without a radio or any other accessory: that would have been vulgar. It wasn't far from the hill where the villa stood to Inverigo, but in no time at all after Davide had sat down behind the wheel, Duca saw the villa rise up into the sky, then the road below almost hit him in the face, there were a series of jolts, blinding lights, presumably the lights of the other cars, and the Giulietta stopped: they had arrived.

'Your father told me how fast you drive,' he said, 'but he didn't tell me how well.' The road was narrow and full of bends, and there was a lot of traffic at this time of year: you had to be a really good driver to do that journey so quickly.

He continued working on his difficult patient, but it was like trying to make friends with a blank, talking into a void, coaxing a desert. Davide never spoke of his own accord, he only answered questions, and where possible answered only 'yes.' First, he took him to the bar. 'Go ahead and have a whisky, we'll start the treatment tomorrow.'

The place, which, like the villa, was on the side of a hill, had pretentions to being a nightclub, though it was more like a dance hall. The dance floor was on a veranda overlooking the garden. It was almost empty, a few couples of modest weekday sinners could be seen in the dim lighting. For the moment, two young people were dancing to the music of the jukebox. According to a poster, a fabulous orchestra would be playing at ten o'clock, which rather suggested about fifty musicians, but there were only four instruments on the stand.

On a little terrace there were a few laid tables: that was the restaurant. In less than an hour they ate ham that tasted of the refrigerator, chicken in aspic which by way of contrast was very well cooked, and a mediocre capricciosa salad. The best thing was the mild, slightly damp air and the view, through the darkness, of all those dots of light, houses and cottages and street lamps, sloping down towards the Milanese plain.

Davide ate, but it was clear he was making an effort, he hadn't drunk even half a glass of wine, and he wasn't speaking, so before he finished the salad Duca stood up, went to the bar and found three kinds of whisky. He brought the three bottles back to the table. 'Choose the kind you prefer, I don't mind which one.'

'Neither do I.'

'Then we'll keep the biggest bottle. I didn't ask for ice or soda because I didn't think you needed them.'

'I always drink it straight.'

'So do I.' He poured some whisky into Davide's wine glass. 'From now on, any time you want a drink, help yourself. I'm absent-minded, and besides, I have a lot of things to talk to you about.'

And he resumed his questions, which was the only way to talk to his companion, the only way to get a few sentences out of him. Every now and again he would ask a question, and every now and again Davide would reply, and every now and again the music of the band would drift through from the dance floor, and there were actually stars over the little terrace.

Yes, his mother was very tall, that was the answer to one question. His mother was from Cremona, another answer. No, he didn't like the sea, but his mother did, she liked it a lot, they had a house in Viareggio but since his mother's death they had only been there once; no, he'd never had a steady girlfriend: this was in answer to the question, 'Can you tell me about your first girlfriend?'

'Steady is just a manner of speaking,' Duca insisted, 'a girl to go out with for a few days, a week.'

Answer: 'No.'

It was a bit tiresome. Duca poured Davide a drink: stoically, once the first round was over, he hadn't served himself again, and he almost over-filled the young man's glass. 'It isn't good, but this way we spare ourselves the trouble of pouring twenty times. Then maybe you'll contribute a bit to the conversation. I want to talk about women, and not just talk about them. The last time I touched a girl's arm was forty-one months ago. I woke up next to her and realised I had my hand on her arm, she was still asleep, then she woke up and took her arm away. Since then forty-one months have passed. I don't think I can carry on any longer with this involuntary abstinence.' If he did, he felt he would end up in the same kind of bunker in which Davide had taken refuge.

'You may not have much luck here,' Davide said. Coming from him, it was quite a long sentence.

'I don't know, I'm going to see.' He left him alone on the little terrace under the stars and walked through the bar to the dance floor. It had filled up a little, and there weren't many men, although the few there were were making quite a racket. He examined the refined young ladies one by one: the ones from Milan all had companions and were all got up to look like Princess Soraya, the others had a homely air, with plastic necklaces, hairdos done by their apprentice hair-dresser friends, and weird gold-coloured sandals. But he had long ago stopped believing in that homely air. He went back to the little terrace, where he was pleased to see that Davide had finished his glass of whisky, and led him to the dance floor. He wasn't swaying much more than before; once you've had a certain amount of alcohol, you either regain your balance or fall asleep.

'I can't dance,' Davide said. They sat down at a table a long way from the band, in one of the most private and least well-lit corners of the place.

'Well, I dance very well.' Having satisfied the eager waiter with an order of whisky, he stood up and went and asked one of the girls for a dance: one of the homeliest, she wasn't even wearing make-up. At the end of the dance, the girl accepted an orange juice at their table. 'I can't stay very late. My father lets me stay out until eleven, I can go home at midnight, but if he wakes up I'll be for it.'

'What a pity,' he said. 'My friend has a villa here, and he has a hi-fi and some wonderful records.'

At the word 'villa' the girl turned pensive, he took her back onto the dance floor as soon as the band struck up again and spoke to her gently. She seemed like the kind of girl who could understand the aspirations of two men alone on a starry night like tonight, and by the end of the dance she had agreed to two things: she would come to the villa, and she would bring along a friend.

'But you'll have to take us home early, half-past at the most,' she insisted, somewhat unwillingly. She had even extended her schedule by half an hour.

It didn't take long for the friend to appear, the girl was away for three minutes and came back with another girl just like her, they seemed like two suits of the same cut, one of one colour and the other of another, because the first was blonde, the second was a brunette. Their resemblance wasn't so much physical, or in the clothes they wore, it was a spiritual resemblance. They both approved his buying a number of small bottles, they were pleased with the Giulietta, and got ready to make conversation during the ride, but at a hundred and twenty kilometres an hour on that road it was beyond them and they didn't catch their breaths until they pulled up outside the villa. 'I don't like going so fast,' the brunette said: her name was apparently Mariolina, or was Mariolina the other one? 'Please drive slower on the way back, or we'll have to walk.'

Davide didn't sway again for the rest of the party, he was just a little stiff, and didn't speak, Duca was the one who did the talking, because when you devote yourself to socially redeeming work you have to see it through to the end, isn't that true, Dr. Duca Lamberti—shake of the head—and you, Dr. Duca Lamberti—shake of the head—are the prince of socially redeeming work, nay, the duke, Duca meant duke, didn't it, ah, what a sense of humour: yes, he could liberate mankind, embodied for the moment by Davide Auseri, from the scourge of alcoholism; he could liberate mankind from the fear of death, mankind in that case in the form of Signora Sofia Maldrigati whose eyes went purple with terror as soon as the consultant who told dirty jokes came anywhere near her; he could liberate anyone, from any ills, liberation was his profession, and he spoke for almost an hour to the girls and to Davide, he tried to get the hi-fi to work but it was broken and then one of the girls switched on the radio to Roma 2, and he continued speaking, like a presenter now, with dance music in the background.

As he poured the drinks, he told the girls that his friend's name was Davide and that he was a mute. The girls behaved themselves and didn't drink too much, the things they told the two men about themselves were somewhat unlikely, but he and Davide accepted these things as if they believed them, and so they all managed to make this little get-together seem not at all vulgar, until Duca took Mariolina aside for a few moments, assuming that it was Mariolina, and explained the situation.

A few minutes later, Mariolina managed to get Davide up out of his armchair and walked sinuously up the stairs with him towards the sleeping quarters on the first floor: even with her high heels and her hairdo she didn't come up to his shoulder. Once the two young lovers had disappeared,

Duca stretched out on the sofa; the other girl, softened up by the music and a couple of drinks, sat down on the floor next to him, and, with her long hair around her face, turned into a sophisticated Françoise Hardy, murmuring the lyrics of a sad song. Then she broke off and said, more concretely and clearly, although passionately, 'Well, here we are, is there somewhere we can go, too?' And she turned her gaze towards the upper floor, hoping there was also a bed for her.

He poured her another drink, and drank some more himself. He couldn't tell the girl that prolonged abstinence generates a kind of mental block, an adjustment to the state of chastity. Basically, chastity was just another vice: once you start being chaste, you can't get out of the habit and you become even more chaste. But after a question like that from a woman, especially in Italy, a rejection, however skilfully done, was impossible. An honest, conscientious tramp like this Françoise Hardy, who had honestly agreed to keep him company, would never understand: she'd be offended, she'd think he was a cripple, in every sense of the word, she might even think he was queer. He didn't want to upset such a nice girl from the nice Brianza. 'It's better here, but turn off the radio.' There had been a high-ranking Fascist official during the Spanish Civil War who had liked to make love to a record of Ravel's *Bolero*: Duca didn't want to get to that point.

About 1:30, with great refinement, Mariolina came downstairs, alone. Duca and Françoise Hardy had switched the radio on again and, with great refinement, were trying to seem like good friends. Before Mariolina could get all the way downstairs, he went to her and gently sat her down on the bottom step, sat down next to her and requested a friendly explanation. The questions he asked her were very indiscreet, but the girl was intelligent in her way, and he appealed to her sense of understanding.

At question number 1, which was one of the less indelicate, the girl laughed out loud. 'I also thought he'd fall asleep afterwards, but he didn't, quite the contrary.'

Question number 2 was more indelicate, and the girl simply answered, 'No.'

She also answered no to questions 3, 4, and 5. Her friend brought a drink over for her and clearly wanted to stay there, listening, but after hearing questions 6 and 7, and Mariolina's answers, she seemed offended by their indecency and went back to the sofa next to the radio.

Question number 8 was the last one and Mariolina replied, almost moved, 'No, he didn't do that, he switched on the little radio next to the bed, and that was the only light in the room.' She liked describing the scene: it must have impressed her. 'He lit a cigarette for me and apologised for not speaking very much, then he asked me if I wanted to spend the night here or if I preferred to be taken home. I told him that I had to go home, I went in the bathroom and when I came back he was already dressed, trousers, shirt, shoes, and he apologised again.'

'What for?'

'For not taking me back himself, he told me he felt uncomfortable.'

'Uncomfortable about what?'

'About seeing you again.'

The psychosexual investigation was over. Even from that

point of view Michelangelo's David was perfectly normal. Boringly normal. The eight technical and analytical questions he had asked Mariolina had received unequivocal answers. Davide Auseri was a vigorous young man, with an old-fashioned craving for the opposite sex, and without any abstract desires or variants that would have been anomalous for someone of his age. The alcohol, even the high volume he was consuming, had not yet had any effect: there was no failure or irregularity, Mariolina's expert testimony had been specific on this point.

He got up from the bottom step and helped his sexual informant to her feet. 'One quick drink, and home we go.'

A few of the banknotes Engineer Auseri had given him were discreetly transferred from his jacket pocket into the girls' handbags, but then the whole evening had had a tone of refinement about it. Duca dropped the girls outside the restaurant under the stars where they had been picked up, and which was still open, and then drove slowly back to the villa in the Giulietta. At the gate, he was met by a distinguished-looking old gentleman wearing a raincoat over his long nightshirt, who informed him in perfect Italian without even the slightest trace of dialect that he was the butler, apologised for his attire, and told him that he had been asked by young Signor Auseri to show him to his room and provide him with anything he needed for the night.

The cinematic butler led him to the first floor and showed him his room, as well as the bathroom, which he already knew, and after a deferential bow, one hand over his heart to keep his raincoat closed, left him alone.

The room was next door to Davide's. The layout of the

house wasn't hard to grasp: this was probably the room Engineer Auseri slept in when he came here. Not only was this logical, it was confirmed by the books on a shelf on the wall. There were two histories of the Second World War, a history of the Republic of Salò, a history of Italy from 1860 to 1960, *Human Knowledge* by Bertrand Russell, a sales brochure in English about non-flammable paint, and issues of the Touring Club's travel magazine in a couple of binders. Constructive reading for a well-constructed mind like Auseri's.

He hadn't brought any luggage with him, not knowing when he had left Milan that he would be staying here. It didn't matter. In the bathroom, he put a little toothpaste on his tongue and rinsed his mouth, quickly performed his ablutions, and went back to his room wearing nothing but his pants. He wasn't feeling very happy.

Warm gusts of damp air came in through the window, along with a few mosquitoes, but above all a heavy silence, because there were no more cars passing on the road beneath the villa. His unhappiness increased when, despite his having washed himself, he found a long hair belonging to Françoise Hardy on his neck. In prison, too, these hours in the dead of night had been difficult ones to get through. He was ready for the onslaught of thoughts and memories, but when the wave arrived, it engulfed him, it was even worse than he had feared. But there was nothing he could do.

He had got everything wrong.

3

His first mistake had been to hate the director of the clinic. True, everything about Arquate was hateful—his physical appearance, like a horse dealer disguised as a surgeon, his character, the tone of his voice, his rude manner—but hate is pointless. If he didn't like Arquate, he should just have left the clinic.

But hating Arquate as he did, he had been wrong to place so much weight on what happened that morning. Arquate and he had just left Signora Maldrigati's room, after a purely routine visit, and Arquate, leaving the door open—he never closed doors, it was a matter of principle with him—had said, 'The woman may be on my hands until the August bank holiday, or just after. They always seem to be on the verge but they never go.' His voice, already as loud as a sports commentator's, had boomed even more than usual because he was annoyed. Not only Signora Maldrigati, the poor lady in question, but all the patients in the clinic must have heard his words.

The reason for this annoyance was that every year from 5 to 20 August, Professor Arquate closed his small but busy clinic and sent the patients home, either declaring them suddenly cured or assuring them that they needed a change of air. He couldn't always empty the clinic by the date fixed by him, or rather fixed by his wife, who needed to be in Forte dei Marmi by that date, because every year one of her sisters arrived from New York to spend her holidays with her; and when, because of a patient, he had to postpone the date, which meant quarrelling with his wife, Arquate got annoyed.

Duca shouldn't have become so indignant at those words, or been so upset by the desperation of Signora Maldrigati, who had heard them. Both reactions had been serious mistakes.

Signora Maldrigati had heard the words, she had understood them perfectly, and had entered into a phase of terror. She moaned for a whole half-day, injections didn't calm her down, only the strongest sedatives at last plunged her into a deep, desperate sleep. She had never been under the illusion that she still had a long time to live, but the great physician's words had told her just how little time she had: she would be dead even before the August holiday, which was what Arquate hoped, or if not, then soon after it.

He should have let her be. It was a distressing case but not uncommon: thanks to the morphine Signora Maldrigati wasn't in any pain, all he had to do was let the nurse get on with giving her the injections. Instead of which, he had stayed with her as much as he could and tried to convince her it wasn't true that she was about to die. Another mistake, because, old and riddled with cancer as Signora Maldrigati might be, she was an intelligent woman.

At the trial, he had been asked how long it was after Signora Maldrigati asked him to help her die that he had agreed to give her the fatal injection of ircodine.

He had made the mistake of answering, 'All through the morning of 30 July she kept begging me to let her die.' He shouldn't have mentioned the dates, should have kept everything vague, as if he couldn't remember.

'And when did you give her the ircodine injection?'

He had made the mistake of giving the chilling answer, 'The night of 31 July to 1 August.'

'In other words,' the prosecutor had said, 'you took the decision to kill a sick old woman, albeit under the specious name of euthanasia, in a mere thirty-six hours. Any soul-searching you may have done about the morality of killing a human being who might still have lived several more years lasted no more than thirty-six hours, or even less, because you must have slept for seven or eight of those hours.'

Ever since, he had been unable to silence that voice in his mind, but only because of the stupidity of what it was saying. Before the trial he had believed there must be a limit to stupidity, then he had realised he had been wrong even about that. Only the skill of the lawyer his father had provided for him had saved him, at least partly, from all the mistakes he had made: three years' imprisonment and being struck off the register wasn't too bad. He could have got fifteen years, just for making sure that Signora Maldrigati was relieved of the terror of death. Dying is a hundred times better than being afraid of dying, as he had tried—ridiculously—to explain at the trial, standing suddenly and crying out, 'Signora Maldrigati's eyes turned purple as soon as she saw Professor Arquate, after he had let her know the date of her death . . .' The two carabinieri had made him sit down again, and as soon as sentence was pronounced, Signora Maldrigati's niece had gone to the notary to talk about the inheritance.

His father had visited him in prison one morning, but had left again almost immediately because he had not felt well. Four days later, he had suffered a fatal heart attack. Left alone during those three years, Duca's sister Lorenza had met a kind gentleman who had shown an interest in her and comforted her and got her pregnant, at which point he had told her he was married and promptly vanished from her life. Lorenza had asked Duca if he liked the name Sara for the child. From prison he had answered yes. How wrong it had all been.

And he was wrong, too, in not wanting to take sleeping pills, because he could have avoided staying awake until dawn and hearing Arquate's voice or his father's, or Signora Maldrigati's moans, which only the ircodine had mercifully silenced forever. In prison, too, the doctor had offered him pills, but he had refused. Anyone might have thought the reason he couldn't sleep was because of his remorse over killing a sick woman who might have lived several more years. But it was idiotic to think that Signora Maldrigati could have lived for more than a month or two at the most, it was only at the trial that anyone had thought of saying that. The reason he couldn't sleep was simply that he didn't like the world around him any more. Even a hen can find it hard to sleep in a henhouse it isn't really happy about.

It was only four, but the wave started to recede inside him, maybe the usual nocturnal torture was coming to an end. A little earlier, he had heard a noise, it might have been a door being closed slowly, or a window. Michelangelo's David was probably also having difficulty sleeping: the world he was in couldn't be too pleasant either. Duca got up to fetch a book. He chose one at random, which turned out to be the history of the republic of Salò, and equally at random he read a memo from Buffarini to Mussolini: the enthusiasm of the Italian people for the war had been cooling rapidly since Stalingrad and the allied landings in Morocco, the Duce had to remember that the spirit of the population was quite different from the days of the Empire. Even their hostility towards their German comrades was increasing . . .

He closed the book abruptly, got up, and put it back on the shelf. At that moment there was something he didn't like in the house, any more than he liked the streak of grey in the dawn sky. He left the room, as if he already knew what it was that he didn't like, even though he didn't, and knocked at the door of the next room, Davide's room.

No answer. He tried to turn the handle: the door was locked. All at once, he realised what had happened and pounded with his fist, three or four times. 'Open up, or I'll knock the door down.'

No sound, for a moment, he pounded again, more loudly, and as he pounded the key turned in the lock and the door opened. It was as he had feared. With his right hand Davide was holding a handkerchief over his left wrist, the handkerchief was already soaked with blood, it was trickling down. The most distressing way to die.

Duca didn't say anything, just pushed Davide into the bathroom. There was a first aid case on the wall which, quite unusually, contained everything he needed. With his huge arm stretched over the wash basin, Davide let him do whatever he wanted. He had known what he was doing when he slit his wrist, had known what he was aiming for: the greatest

loss of blood with the smallest cut. That made it easier for
Duca to stitch and dress the wound, and less than half an
hour later the would-be suicide was lying on his bed. The
cuff of his shirt hid most of the bandage. He hadn't said a
word so far and, lying like that on the bed, still wasn't saying anything.

Duca hadn't said a word either. Not one. As soon as he
had put him back on the bed he looked for the stash of
whisky. It was child's play: the only place a person as tall
as Davide Auseri could hide a bottle was on top of the
wardrobe; by standing on tiptoe he managed to reach that
obvious hiding place and took down the bottle. He laughed
nervously to himself: he wasn't much shorter than Davide.

He started to drink from the bottle: one sip, then a breath,
another longer sip, another breath, the third sip, enough
now. He needed it, he was still frozen with terror, and even
the whisky didn't warm him up very much. He put the bottle
back on top of the wardrobe, sat down on Davide's bed and
looked at him. His expression was normal, he hadn't cried,
he wasn't pale, the skin of his face was dry. That was the terrible thing about it: he had decided quite calmly and lucidly
that he wanted to die. At the age of twenty-two.

'Don't you ever think of other people?' Duca asked. He
looked at the window: the square of sky was milky with
dawn. No answer. 'No, I'm not talking about your father,
the grief you'd have given your father if you'd died. I'm talking about other people, anyone, someone you might pass
in the street. Me, for example. Suppose I hadn't heard that
noise just now: it was you going into the bathroom to get

the scissors to slit your wrists. Suppose I'd been asleep, and
when I woke up I'd found you, having already bled to death.
Imagine my situation. I just got out of prison, only three days
ago, I was sent there for an offence that some people called
homicide, although with extenuating ideological circumstances. This morning they find me here, with a dead young
man, after a night spent with women of easy virtue, the
remains of our orgy still downstairs. You have no idea how
imaginative the press can be, or how suspicious the police.
They would have talked about drugs, and as a former doctor
I'd have been accused of organising the whole sadistic party
and providing heroin, cocaine, mescaline, marijuana: they
might have found your suicide suspicious. "Someone cut
his veins for him while he was in a drugged stupor": there's
always a lawyer ready to make that kind of accusation in
court. So I'd have immediately gone back inside, and would
have been ruined forever. Now listen to me: it's true that you
barely know me, but I have a sister who's twenty-two, with
an illegitimate one-year-old daughter, and their lives depend
entirely on me. If I work they eat, if I don't they have to live
on charity, as they did all the time I was in prison. If this
stupid joke of yours of trying to die had succeeded, it would
have been all over for me. I know you couldn't have thought
of these things, but I do, the reason I didn't strangle you as
soon as I saw you with your wrist cut was because I still have
a lot of self-control.'

At last a word, just one, a brief one, bland and yet moving: 'Sorry,' and his eyes narrowed a little as he said it:
Davide, too, had a lot of self-control.

'Don't do it again, Davide'—he had never before threatened a fellow man like this—'I can't watch over you every instant and a person who wants to do himself in will manage it even with ten guards watching him. If you're tired of life, wait till I've finished my job, in a month you'll be drinking only mineral water, then I'll go and you'll be able to do whatever you like. But as long as I'm here with you,' he grabbed the collar of his open shirt with one hand and, heavy as he was, lifted him until he was almost sitting up, and they were almost eye to eye, 'as long as I'm here with you, you won't do things like that, I'd stop you, but then I'd kill you myself, and I wouldn't be gentle.'

However intelligent he was, the young man didn't realise how much play-acting there was in this scene. Duca was exaggerating in order to give him a moral reason not to kill himself, he had given him a dramatic explanation of the way his suicide would have cruelly ruined a man, a man like him, even though he barely knew him. Sometimes, at the age of twenty-two, an appeal to your sense of morality actually works.

'It won't happen again,' Davide said, narrowing his eyes even more: he must have been extremely unhappy, but he managed to hide it almost completely.

Duca stood up. He was still in his pants. 'I'm going to get my cigarettes.' He went back to his room and got dressed: the wonderful new shirt, the wonderful blue suit of ultra-light material, the fantastic light blue tie, all given to him on coming out of prison by Lorenza or, more correctly, by Superintendent Carrua who had given her the money. His hair was only two millimetres high and didn't need combing, but as he knotted his tie in front of the wardrobe mirror he realised that he needed a shave. He lit a cigarette and went back to Davide's room.

It was still only dawn, daylight was a long time coming, but he didn't need the light on any more and he switched it off. Davide was still there, monumental and unhappy, lying on a bed that was too short and too narrow for him, as if lying on a plank. Duca took a chair and moved it close to him. He kept smoking his cigarette, without offering him one.

'I haven't asked you why you tried to kill yourself, because you wouldn't have told me.' He didn't wait for a reply, he knew there wouldn't be one, he took a few more puffs of his cigarette, then said, 'And I'm not going to ask you now, because you still wouldn't tell me.'

In fact, he didn't say anything at all. But Duca had understood. The question was not the drinking, the alcoholism, as Davide's father the emperor thought. Parents always think their children are still at the lullaby stage. For a young man of that age to have such a clear-headed desire to die, the reason had to be a deep and serious one. Davide was a healthy young man, from every point of view, Mariolina and company had confirmed that, and for a healthy young man to consciously resolve on his own death, there must have been a painful wound to his ego. A simple event, however serious, wouldn't have reduced him to this: even if he had killed someone, if he had set fire to an old lady or put a bomb in the basement of Milan Central Station, he wouldn't have acted like this. Davide Auseri had been destroyed by something. Or by someone. That was what he had to discover. The drinking was a laughable matter.

'And now that you're rested, let's go.' He stood up and threw the cigarette end out of the window, which was still milky with dawn, neither more nor less than before, as if the dawn had come to a halt. Even stranger, there was no dawn chorus. It was just as silent as it had been in the middle of the night. 'This isn't the right place for you or for me. Let's go straight away. I'll pack your bag for you: for a couple of days it's best that you use your left arm as little as possible. I don't think you're sleepy. Neither am I.'

Getting the necessary indications from Davide, he found a beautiful soft suitcase, dark blue, obviously, and put in it everything they would need. Then, with toilet paper he scrupulously cleaned the bloodstains that led from the room all the way to the bathroom—to support Lorenza and his niece he would have to do this and more—and when everything was ready he said, 'Now you can get up. I may have missed a few bloodstains, so before leaving, wake the maid, the butler, whoever you like, and tell them you're going, then even if they discover the bloodstains I missed they won't think there's been a murder and we ran away.'

Davide obeyed him promptly and gloomily, he woke the butler who had appeared in his nightshirt the previous night, had him take the case out to the car and sat down quietly next to Duca at the wheel, knowing already that he wouldn't be the one to drive.

So they descended from the soft hills of the Brianza into

the Milanese plain and near Monza they found somewhere open: obviously it didn't have any drinkable whisky, it wasn't so much a bar, more a kind of shed, but Michelangelo's David was starting to turn pale and need refuelling. Duca ordered two grappas. Davide drank his straight down, so Duca passed him his own glass.

'The treatment starts now,' he said. 'Whenever I think you really need a drink, I'll give you one. Otherwise not a drop, and I'll stop you any way I can.'

Davide drank the second glass, too, they were so small, so measly, so reminiscent of an earlier time, a world of rose-petal cordials and shoes with heeltaps, that Duca said, 'Have another one: that's an order.' He got back behind the wheel and after a while looked at Davide: his pallor had gone, his breathing had got back to normal. It wasn't the derisory loss of blood that had made him sick, obviously. It was the cobra he had inside him, which was eating him up.

'If you tell me what happened to you, and let me help you, it'll be much better for you,' Duca said. He wasn't expecting any reply. And he didn't get one.

4

Even in Milan, the sun rises every now and again. It had risen that morning, there was a reddish glow on the top floors of the buildings, people were already panting with the heat. He parked the Giulietta in the Piazza Leonardo da Vinci. 'Let's go and see my sister. She should be awake, the baby has her first feed at six.'

The mammoth fifteenth-century door, in marked contrast to the modesty of the building, was closed, but he didn't even look at the door, he whistled and Lorenza appeared at the window on the first floor with her child in her arms.

'I didn't think I'd heard right, I wasn't expecting you at this hour,' Lorenza said, throwing him down the keys.

'This is a friend of mine, make us some coffee.' He led Davide up the short flight of stairs. 'The apartment is old and small, and has a double supply of cockroaches, they come in from the street and also the courtyard. We won't be here long, though.'

Lorenza was on the landing, with the child in her arms. She was in dark pyjamas and her shoulder-length hair was gathered into a ponytail by a common elastic band.

Duca took the child in his arms and made the introductions, by pure chance Sara wasn't soaking wet. 'Has she already done it or is she about to?' he asked Lorenza.

'She's done it, I only just changed her.' Lorenza's dark eyes were looking at him happily, she even looked happily at Davide. It was her way of looking at life: even when she came to see him in prison she looked at him like that, she talked to him like that, in that happy voice: 'The lawyer says everything's going to be fine.'

'Then I'll hold her, and come with you to the kitchen while you make the coffee.' He turned to Davide, who was sitting motionless on a rickety chair. 'Excuse me, Davide, I'll be right back.' In the kitchen, he walked up and down with Sara in his arms: she was a quiet child, as long as she was in someone's arms, otherwise she screamed as if her throat was being cut.

'My cigarettes are in the right-hand pocket of my jacket.' Lorenza took them out, lit one, and put it between his lips.

'In the left-hand pocket I have a cheque and some money. Take all the money and leave me the cheque.'

As she took all the notes from his jacket pocket, Lorenza turned pensive. She put them in a drawer in the kitchen table and lit the gas under the already prepared coffee maker. 'What is this, Duca?'

'It's an advance for my job.' He blew the smoke in the opposite direction from the child. 'It's a job I'm able to do, don't worry, Carrua found it for me. I may not be able to come and see you for a while, that's why I came today.' And also to give her the money: on the baby's high chair there was a roll, a sign that Lorenza had not been able to buy the Plasmon biscuits she usually got.

'But what is it you have to do?' Lorenza had become more fearful about things since Duca had been in prison, since their dad had died, since she had found herself alone and the doctor had told her one day that in his opinion she was pregnant. Fear made her large, beautiful mouth narrow a little.

Without going into too much detail, he explained what he was supposed to do with the young man who was in the other room, and they went back in there with the coffee and found him where they had left him. Duca kept the child in his arms for the rest of the visit, it was a risk because if Sara decided to pass water it could well ruin his new suit, his only suit, but Sara's little hand around his neck and the other hand feeling for his nose, her laughing blue eyes, her stammering of a few syllables, were worth it: it was a calculated risk. In the meantime he was watching Davide, but there wasn't much to see. The lack of alcohol made him even more alien to this everyday world. He had even stopped answering questions, except with a smile or a nod of the head, and he was also a little pale: he would need refuelling again before he lapsed into another depressive state.

'We're going.' He gave Sara back to his sister, completely dry.

'When will you be back?' Lorenza asked.

'Hard to say. I'll phone you.' In the car he said to Davide, 'Hold on a while longer. We're going to the barber now, then we'll go to a good bar near here.' Davide smiled, and gave a little nod of gratitude. At the barber's Duca had a shave, too. They sat next to each other, and in the mirror he saw Davide half close his eyes every now and again: if he fell asleep it would be a blessing.

He fell asleep.

'Psst.' Duca spoke under his breath to the barber. 'We've been driving all night, he's tired and not feeling very well. Let him sleep, at least until it gets busy.'

'It won't get busy today.' The barber was an understanding man, a man who'd seen everything: he left Davide with lather on half his face and lit a cigarette.

Duca had his own hair cut by the barber's assistant, a young man from Como who, unlike the barber, had seen nothing and had never predicted, among the many events that might occur in the world, the possibility of a man falling asleep at the barber's, although, he said in a low voice, he himself had once fallen asleep in a café in Como, which was so unlike him that he would remember it for the rest of his life.

With his hair cut and his beard shaved, he started talking to the old barber, looking every now and again at his watch and every now and again at Davide: every minute that passed was a minute less to drink alcohol and a minute more to get reorganised. Perhaps he would sleep until midday, but at 10:15 an old customer came in, a noisy Milanese, the very kind who finds so much success on television, a thin bony man, vaguely hateful for his vulgarity and his wine-red face, who yelled out a Fascist slogan as he entered.

So Davide woke up, realised that he had been asleep, and on the cheek that was free of lather Duca could see the red mark, but the old barber knew his job, he was ready, he finished shaving him and they left.

'Sorry I took you there,' Duca said, 'your usual hairdresser's may be a more pleasant place.' He got no answer. He pulled up outside a bar in the Via Plinio. 'This is the best bar in the area. Order whatever you like.'

He didn't look at Davide as he drank a double whisky, but only said, 'Drink slowly, I'm not in any hurry.'

The sleep and the whisky had revived Davide a little. Back in the car, he said, 'I must be quite a burden to you.'

'A bit,' Duca said, driving. 'But I like you.' Reaching the Piazza Cavour, he turned into the Via Fatebenefratelli, and parked in the Via dei Giardini. 'Wait for me here. I have to go to Police Headquarters. I'll leave the car keys, but remember what I told you this morning: don't do anything stupid as long as I'm with you. If you're not here when I get back, I'll come looking for you, and I hope for your sake I find you already dead, because I don't rate your chances if I find you alive. And don't start drinking again.'

Davide nodded his head several times, without smiling. He would be there when Duca got back: he was an honest young man.

As Duca entered Headquarters, the memory of his father hit him like a punch, and a black veil fell over him. Whenever, as a boy, he had come in with his father through that door, crossed that courtyard, climbed those stairs, walked through that corridor and, in the little room, not much more than a cubbyhole, that his father called an office, his father raised his left arm when he could, in other words, not very much after the stab wound he'd got in Sicily, and pointed to the chair, as if it actually was a chair rather than a little bench with a plank as a back and said to him, 'Sit there and study,' he would place on his knees the schoolbook that his father had told him to bring, and start to read and reread, and when he needed to write, his father would lend him a corner of his own little table, which passed, however improbably, as a desk. In that way, in that place, he had studied many aspects of infinitesimal calculus, chemistry, and even projective geometry.

But this morning he walked along a different corridor, a more silent, deserted one, there was only one officer outside the door of Carrua's office. A new officer who, before letting him in, wanted a lot of explanation and looked as if he might want to search him. In the end, Carrua himself came out, shouting.

'You let in all kinds of nuisances I don't want to see and when a friend of mine comes you keep them outside.' Carrua may never have spoken normally, he either shouted or kept silent. 'How did it go with Auseri?' he screamed at Duca as soon as they were inside the office.

He told him how it had gone and thanked him for finding him the job. 'It's quite an unusual job, but I like it, even though it's not very clear-cut.'

'What's not very clear-cut about it?'

'I find it hard to believe it's all about a young man who drinks. There must be something else.'

'What kind of thing?'

'I don't know. The kind that might also be of interest to the police.'

Silence. Superintendent Luigi Carrua was looking at him. He was an old friend of his father's, Duca must have been five or six years old the first time he had looked at him, and since then they had met on thousands of occasions and Carrua had looked at him thousands of times, but he still couldn't get used to that look: when Carrua looked at you, you felt naked. He was short, not fat, weighed down by thirty years of police work, even though grey his hair was long and neatly back-combed, without a receding hairline, and he looked more like a bank official than a police officer. Except when he stared into your eyes. 'If you take after your father,' he said in an unusually low voice, 'then maybe there *is* something. Your father was never wrong.' He raised his voice again. 'But you're a doctor, not a policeman. The Auseris would never have anything to do with the police.' The telephone rang, he picked it up and listened, then shouted again, 'All right, let them do the post-mortem again, I'm not the bloody sawbones.' He turned back to Duca and shrugged. 'They still say Superintendent Carrùa. That was another one. They've known me for ten years and every day I tell them: Càrrua, please, with the stress on the first *a*, not Carrùa with the stress on the *u*, but it never works: Carrùa is what they have in their heads and Carrùa is what they say.'

He smiled. The man's one weakness was the correct pronunciation of his name: it was his secret wound and one that seemed likely never to heal, because people instinctively said Carrùa and it never even occurred to them that they should be pronouncing it Càrrua. He became serious again, he seemed upset.

No, Duca didn't like the job. 'If, while looking after this young man, I end up discovering something not entirely above board, what should I do? Engineer Auseri is your friend.'

The shout this time was more forceful. 'You won't discover anything because there's nothing to discover about Auseri. We were at school together, we did our military service together, we're growing old together in this filthy world, he has a son who's a bit backward, but who won't even step off the pavement if the light isn't green. Auseri's son drinks because he's backward, that's all. But you, being the intelligent man you are, will teach him to prefer lemon juice.'

Then Duca laid it out for him clearly, because what was the point in life of being the son of a policeman, or the protégé of a highly placed official in Headquarters, if the wheels got jammed and you were crushed anyway? They had got jammed with Signora Maldrigati, and he didn't want to be crushed again. 'Listen to me. Maybe I won't discover anything, which will be better for me, but if I discover the slightest thing, I'll come here and bring it to you on a silver platter and resign from this job. I don't want to have anything to do with people or things that are outside the law. That's not an excessive demand, is it?'

Instead of the shouting he was expecting, silence. For a long time. Then Carrua stood up abruptly and at last screamed, 'You must have a reason to think there's something there that's outside the law.'

'I didn't want to tell you, because maybe it isn't a reason,' he replied loud and clear, 'but last night your friend's son tried to kill himself by slitting his wrists. I found him just in time. He's outside right now, alive and well, waiting for me. But a young man that age doesn't try to die if there isn't some underlying cause.'

'And didn't he tell you why?'

'No, just as for the past year he hasn't told his father why he drinks like that, without any friends or acquaintances driving him to it. And the more I asked him, the less he would tell me.'

'A lot of people kill themselves for no reason.'

'Davide Auseri isn't a young girl who's been seduced. He may be young, but he's a man. And he isn't backward, as you think, or as his father thinks. If he wants to die he has a serious reason, and serious reasons, for a man, always have something to do with the law. I've already had enough dealings with the law. Which is why I've come here to tell you that, if there's something not right about this, I'm dropping everything.'

No shouting. Carrua sat down again. 'You're right.' He had grown sad. He had done everything he could to help Duca, to protect him, to avoid him being put on trial and going to prison. There had been nothing he could do: the wheels had got jammed. 'I don't think you'll find anything, but if you do, come and tell me straight away and I'll find you another job.' Before opening the door, he gave him a hug. 'Try to hold on. Another year or two, and they'll let you back on the register, everything will be the way it was before, you're still young.'

He let Carrua believe that was what he was hoping for, even though he knew that hope was a kind of secret vice that nobody ever managed to rid themselves of completely.

'Thank you for everything you've done for Lorenza,' he said, hugging him tight.

When he came out into the Via Fatebenefratelli, into the damp sunlight that was as hot as shaving cream from a luxury hairdresser, it struck him that if he didn't find Davide and the Giulietta in the Via dei Giardini, then he had really messed up. But he had had to take the risk: otherwise he would never have known whether he could trust the young man, or what he was made of.

Davide was in his place, walking up and down next to the Giulietta in the incipient shade given by the trees at that hour. Duca saw him from the back, tall, monumental, and felt sorry for him. Whatever the reason, he must be very unhappy. 'Thank you,' he said to him, getting behind the wheel. 'Let's just drop by the bank, and then I'm sorry if I take you somewhere a little sad, but I'm going to see my father's grave.'

At the bank, which was his father's bank, they cashed the cheque he had been given by Engineer Auseri, which was for quite a large amount. They cashed it without any problem, even though they knew he had been in prison and even though his father, with his small savings account, had never done much to boost the institution's profits.

'After we've been to Musocco, we'll stop for a drink,' he told him encouragingly. For the first week he couldn't reduce to less than a third the dose of alcohol Davide was used to drinking, for psychological reasons if for nothing else: he wanted him to stay a normal man, not become a thirsty man who thought of nothing but whisky.

Country graveyards, surrounded by greenery and tall cypresses, are not supposed to be depressing, unlike a large cemetery in a big city which can be quite chilling. But he hadn't yet seen his father's grave, he hadn't even attended the funeral, and now he had in his pocket the sheet of paper Lorenza had given him, on which the numbers of the section and the grave were written, and together with Davide he entered that sad, oceanic expanse which was even more lugubrious in the sun. Of course, the grave was at the far end, and they had to do quite a bit of walking, Duca holding the carnations he had bought at the front gate.

Here was the section, more walking, and here was the grave, much the same as all the others in the row, the extinguished candle in the dark glass, the bed of little flowers scorched by the heat, the spartan inscription, Pietro Lamberti, date of birth and death, and that was it. He laid the carnations, loose, on the flower bed, without any attempt at arranging them artistically. From his photograph, his father looked out stiffly at the world in front of him, and Duca stood stiffly looking at the photograph.

'This is my father,' he said, as if introducing him, 'a police officer, from Emilia Romagna, just like me, but he wasn't typical of the region, he didn't like revolution or revolutionaries, he liked the law, he liked rules. He was absolutely determined to sort out all those who transgressed the law or broke the rules. He was a kind of Javert. He managed to get himself sent to Sicily because he thought he could do something radical to combat the Mafia. For a while the Mafia took no interest in him, they had no time to waste on an ordinary cop, but my father went too far: he managed to get something out of three or four of those peasants who've seen everything and know everything, but always say they know nothing. I don't know what methods he used, maybe he had to bend the rules a little, but in his small way he managed to break through the wall of silence. His superiors promoted him, and the Mafia sent a young man to deal with him: it was a suicide mission, because my father was a very good shot and the attempt didn't succeed, my father shot him dead but not before being stabbed in his left shoulder, his left arm was almost paralysed and he was transferred here to Milan, to a desk job.' He wasn't looking at Davide, he didn't care very much if he was listening or not, he was talking like this as if praying—isn't summing up a man's life a kind of prayer?— but he sensed that Davide was listening, more than that, he had never listened the way he was listening right now.

'Maybe it was because he didn't want the same thing to happen to me that he was against the idea of my becoming a policeman like him, he wanted me to graduate as a doctor, and I did. Nobody will ever know how he managed on a police clerk's salary, and a widower to boot, because my mother died when I was a boy, but the day I graduated he was in bed, suffering with his heart, and when I had my exams, he had his heart attack. Then I did my military service, and by the time I got back, he'd somehow, stuck there in his office in the Via Fatebenefratelli, already found me a place in a clinic, Professor Arquate's clinic. Maybe I'd have worked my way up, and he'd have lived happily to the age of ninety, but I met Signora Maldrigati. She's the old lady

I killed with an injection of ircodine. My father didn't even know the word euthanasia, for him it was worse than if I'd gone mad, or rather, he must have thought I *had* gone mad, and maybe he forgave me because of that, but he realised the consequences of what I had done: I wouldn't be a doctor any more, I'd always have a stain on my record, and that killed him.' His father continued to look at him stiffly from the photograph even when he fell silent, and even if he had heard his words, he still didn't understand why his son had killed, he would never understand it, for all eternity, his look in the photograph said that clearly.

Davide's voice came to him suddenly, in that great heat and sadness, Duca hadn't expected him to be the first to speak. 'I'd like to visit a grave, too.'

Duca nodded, continuing to look at his father.

'But I don't know where it is. It must be here, but I don't know where.'

'There must be an office somewhere,' he said to Davide. He looked at him, only his face was shiny with sweat. 'Just give them the name of the person and they'll tell you the section and the number of the grave.'

Davide's voice remained even. 'It's the woman I killed last year. Her name was Alberta Radelli.'

5

On that stretch of avenue that goes from the Arco della Pace to the Castello Sforzesco, even just after ten in the morning, the sides of the road are lined with alluring female figures, wearing scanty but tight-fitting clothes in summer, who know how to operate in a large metropolis where there are no provincial limits to timetables or conventional divisions between night and day, and at any hour of the day, from midnight to midnight, a citizen can slow down in his car, hail one or other of these ladies, and ask for their co-operation.

A blue Giulietta appeared that morning on the right-hand side of the arch and slowed down, and a woman of forty dressed like a teenage Beatles fan stepped down into the road almost as if to bar the way, but the Giulietta swerved and accelerated, not because Davide Auseri had seen the kind lady and hadn't seen fit to accept what she was offering, but simply because, just as he was about to realise his plan, something inside him almost always drove him to flee. Further on, from behind a tree, a genuine teenager, at any rate a girl no more than twenty, waved him down, as if she had an appointment to present the papers for her marriage. She was blonde, she looked like a gangster's moll in a Hollywood film, or better still, like one of those little girls who, at carnival time, dress up as eighteenth-century ladies for the neighbourhood dance, painted, powdered and completely unaware of the historical aspect of their costumes, concerned only with the fact that they'll be able to eat a lot of sweet things and play a lot of games during the day. But

Davide Auseri swerved away from the blonde, too, as if afraid, even though what he most wanted was to stop. It was almost always like this at first, he was afraid; later, if the girl had managed to get in the car, he wasn't.

But that morning none of the willing ladies standing in the avenue managed to intercept the Giulietta: the fear was stronger, and Davide headed towards the centre, and drove for a long time, feeling quite sad, through the Foro Bonaparte, the Via Dante, the Via Orefici, the Piazza del Duomo, the Corso Vittorio, San Babila, the Corso di Porta Venezia, having no other plan, beyond that failed one, then returned to the Via Palestro, reached the Piazza Cavour and decided to go to the Alemagna in the Via Manzoni to eat something. One instinct having failed him, the instinct for food had returned even more strongly.

He got to the Via dei Giardini and had no difficulty finding somewhere to park the Giulietta because during those scorching August days the metropolis was considered uninhabitable by a large number of its citizens, who, for some reason, found it perfectly habitable in fog, smog, and snow. Even at the Alemagna, he had the place—the bar counter a few dozen metres long for the drinks, a counter a dozen metres long with sandwiches of egg, salmon, caviar, the two counters of pastries and ice cream in quantities reminiscent of Versailles and the Tuileries—almost completely to himself, apart from two other customers who floated like him in the mountain-cold yet unrefreshing air conditioning.

He ate three substantial sandwiches and drank a beer, without daring to look too closely at the five assistants and two cashiers, all women, just as he never looked too closely at anyone, only at inanimate things, provided they weren't dolls or toy dogs with eyes that frightened him as much as human eyes frightened him. However, he did spend some time looking at the assistant on the pastry counter, a specialist in pralines who was somewhat behind with the fashion, with her bouffant hairstyle: the one she wore that day was not the most bouffant, the previous week he had seen one even more bouffant, and the size of that hair suddenly gave him the urge to go back to the park and this time stop. But it was only a sudden whim, the various hidden censors inside him blocked that resurgence of passion and suggested something more spiritual: going to Florence and back, along the Autostrada del Sole, trying to beat his own record of the month before, which was already a very short time. He would eat in Florence and get back to Milan in time for an aperitif. He liked the idea and immediately left the Alemagna.

In the Via dei Giardini, the Giulietta, improbably, was the only car parked in a stretch of about twenty metres near the bus stop. He paid the parking fee to the man in the peaked cap, who immediately walked back into the shade, and he was about to squeeze himself back into his car when he heard that voice.

'Excuse me.'

He turned. A girl in a sky-blue suit, with large, perfectly round dark glasses, was smiling at him, but with a hint of anxiety about her mouth, which apart from her small nose, was the only part of her face that was visible, covered as it was by those large glasses and by her brown hair that descended over her face like two half-closed curtains.

'Excuse me, signore, I've been waiting for a bus for half an hour, I have an important appointment and I'm already late—could you possibly give me a lift to Porta Romana?'

Davide Auseri nodded and opened the door for her. She got in and sat down composedly, placing on her knees a light brown leather handbag which looked more like a large man's wallet, and he set off.

'What street exactly?' he asked.

'Oh, right at the end, if you'd be so kind.'

'Of course, I was going that way myself.'

'I'm so pleased, then I won't be making you waste too much of your time.'

His guest's knees were not completely uncovered, but they were visible and he could look at them as he drove.

'I know it was shameless of me, but you can never find a taxi when you need one.'

Maybe it was her voice that put him on the right track, but not only the voice. He was a solitary man, and solitary men think a lot. Above all, even though he was no expert, he had the impression that the bus that went through the Via dei Giardini didn't go to Porta Romana. And right next to the bus stop there was a taxi stand, and he had seen a long line of them. All the traffic lights in the centre had been on his side, and now he was in the Piazza Missori. The closeness of the girl and the sight of those knees, not to mention the heat, must have made his censors give up the ghost.

'Do you like travelling by car?' he asked her.

'Very much, with a good driver.' Her voice continued to change, its softness had turned inviting.

'I'm going to Florence, along the autostrada. We can be back by six this evening, seven at the latest.'

'Florence is a bit far.' The softness of her voice had diminished a little, but she made no mention of the important appointment she was supposed to have had.

'We'll be back before dinner,' he said. All his censors had vanished by now, and the real Davide Auseri emerged from the depths of his subconscious.

Her voice turned a little harsh. 'I wouldn't like to be dumped in the middle of the road.'

'I don't do things like that.' His voice, too, had turned harsh, it even slightly resembled his father's voice.

The girl took off her glasses and threw back her hair, her eyes were a little tired and a bit afraid, but her expression was sweet, almost innocent, and she said innocently, 'I've always wanted to go to Florence, but going this way is a bit scary.'

A girl who pretends to be waiting for a bus, next to a parking space, and is actually waiting as patiently as a fisherman for whichever man, young or old, comes to collect his car, as long as he's alone and makes it clear he doesn't have any urgent business to attend to, shouldn't be scared of much, but she seemed genuine enough.

'It's the first time someone has ever said they're scared of me.' They were almost at the end of the Corso Lodi and he had to make up his mind. He gently stopped the car and with a distracted, elegant gesture, without showing either wallet or money, managed to take a couple of notes and pass them into the handbag, or wallet, that she was holding on her knees, keeping them clutched in his hand in such a way that the transfer happened without any vulgar banknotes being seen. In many cases, money is a quick-working tranquilliser, an antidote to fears, anxieties, and states of depression. The Davide that had emerged from his subconscious, dripping with instincts, knew that.

'Let's go,' she said, but her voice remained harsh, and even a little bitter now. 'There are lots of ways to get to Florence, clearly I had to go like this.'

Until they got to the tollbooths on the autostrada he drove slowly, and for another ten kilometres or so after taking out the ticket he kept up the same dull pace, but he was just psyching himself up. She had put her glasses on again and let the curtains of her hair fall, and was intelligent enough not to lean on his shoulder. 'Go faster, I like it.'

He humoured her, pushing the Giulietta to its limit, the autostrada was fairly clear, but she didn't see him make even the slightest mistake, or be the slightest bit careless, and despite the figure on the speedometer she didn't have the slightest feeling that she was at risk.

And he didn't say a word. She must know men: she didn't tell him that she really liked driving like this, she didn't tell him anything about herself or ask any questions about him, in short, she had no desire to make conversation, having understood that he was one of those men—maybe they were the best—who do only one thing at a time. For now he was driving, and only driving. She didn't like one-man bands, like those performing dogs that played the drum with sticks tied to their tails, the cymbals with their paws, and bells with their heads. That constant, calm silence was good for Davide, it unblocked him completely, his deepest instincts strained in him like cats closed up in a basket for half a day: hot, aggressive, precise. He wasn't interested any more in whether or not he broke his record from Milan to Florence and back, as his superego had first suggested, and at the service station in Somaglia he stopped outside a hut festively bedecked with flags.

'Let's have a drink.'

Obeying silently, she followed him, they were thirsty and drank a mint cordial, strong and iced.

'Near here there's a nice walk by the river.' He had been here once before, alone, and had realised it was a place that was good for certain things, but he had never thought he'd one day bring a girl here. And yet here he was, with a girl.

Leaving the car in front of the cheerful little hut, they left the area of the service station. There was a road that led to the river, then there was a path that went alongside the river, and then there were tracks that disappeared amid tall bushes and secluded undergrowth. As they walked along the river, she took off her glasses and wiped the lipstick from her lips with a Kleenex, rolled up the little square of soft tissue and threw it in the water: she followed it with her eyes as it floated on the current until he took her by the arm and led her into the bushes.

Being perhaps the more practical of the two, she was the one who chose the place, squatting on the ground in the most sheltered spot. He stood there, smoking a cigarette, and watched her as she took off her sky-blue jacket, under it she had a bra and she took that off, too, and then he, too, took off his jacket, which, outside the house, he only ever took off to make love.

On the way back, she could still see the Kleenex, it had caught in a clump of grass by the water, and she stopped to put on lipstick. 'You're nice,' she said to him as she did so. 'When I saw you in the Via dei Giardini, I wasn't sure whether to approach you, you look like the kind of man who'd ruin a woman, but I needed fifty thousand lire.' She put the lipstick and her mirror back in her handbag and started walking again. 'We can eat here,' she said.

Davide knew he wasn't any good at bargaining, and, still without the vulgarity of any of those ten-thousand-lire notes coming into sight, he transferred from his wallet into her purse, once again, the rest of the sum required to reach the figure she had requested.

'It's too much, I know,' she said. 'Consider it a charitable donation.'

He didn't like talking about money. 'Where are you from?' he asked.

'Naples.'

'You don't sound Neapolitan.'

'I studied elocution for three years, I wanted to work in the theatre, theatre with a capital T. I can recite some Shakespeare, if you like.'

They ate in the festive little hut on the autostrada. They exchanged a bit of superficial, generalised information about themselves: she said vaguely that she had come to Milan almost a year earlier to look for work and hadn't found very much, and he told her he was a clerk in a large office, which was true, after all, he worked for Montecatini, didn't he?

'A well-paid clerk, if you spend like that.' He didn't reply, so she asked him, 'Do you still want to go to Florence and back?'

After the meal, the wild beasts that had defeated the censors in him were even freer. 'I'd prefer to go to the river again,' he said simply.

'So would I,' she replied.

They went to the river again and then came back to have a drink. She was the one who chose whisky: at the time, he preferred beer. After her second whisky he said, 'Isn't all that stuff bad for you?'

'In theory, yes. In practice, as I'm going to kill myself tomorrow, I could drink vitriol now and it wouldn't matter.'

Davide decided, trivially, that the girl was joking and that she had drunk too much, but at the same time he knew he was lying to himself, because deep down he had the feeling that the girl wasn't joking and wasn't drunk, she was a straight person, in her body, her character, and her way of speaking, she never said a superfluous or pointless word: if she wasn't intending to kill herself, she wouldn't have wasted time saying it.

'That's an idea we all get sometimes,' he said.

'Sometimes it isn't only an idea,' she said. 'A few months ago I saw a book displayed in the window of a bookshop. By chance, I read the band across the cover. I can't remember the exact words now, but they were something like: "As soon as I've finished writing this book I'll kill myself." The author, who was a woman, had said that, and having finished the novel she did in fact kill herself. For her, it wasn't just an idea.' They were sitting by the window and every now and again looked through the blinds at the lanes on the autostrada and the cars flashing in the sun like photographers' flashlights. 'For me neither.'

He liked hearing her talk, and he even liked this unexpected topic, Eros and Thanatos are cousins, and he had a few ideas about life and death himself, ideas he'd never been able to talk about due to his lack of social contact, and he told her one now: 'Of course living is difficult, whereas dying is very simple.'

'Yes,' she said, although his observation was not about her. 'But I don't have any desire to die, and never have had. Listen, if I'm not boring you, I'll talk for a few more minutes about personal things, then I'll shut up.'

'I'm not bored at all,' he said, and it was true.

'Anything can happen in life. Today I met you, you may be the man destiny sent me.' Her big wide mouth was brushed at the corners by the curtains of her hair, and she wasn't smiling. 'If you take me away with you, for at least three months, a long way from here, and spend every minute with me, then tomorrow I won't have to kill myself anymore. I know it's absurd, but that's the way things happen to me. If you like me, it won't be hell for you. In appearance—only in appearance—I'm serious, sophisticated, elegant, you can take me anywhere and I won't make you look bad. I know how to eat snails with the correct cutlery, without holding them between my fingers and sucking them as a friend of mine does. Even though you said you're only a clerk, you probably don't need to save money, but if you want to I can live on toast and Coca-Cola and I can sleep in boarding houses. But take me away from Milan for three months, at least three months, it ought to be much longer, maybe a year or two, but three months will do, and then I'll see.'

At that moment, the thought of spending three months with this girl, one girl just for him, something he'd never been able to do because of the network of complexes in which he was imprisoned, opened wide the windows of life for him, and through those windows he saw the three months, verdant, luxuriant, with her naked body gliding softly over those three months, as the car ran on, taking the two of them across an invisible map, Cannes, Paris, Biarritz, Lisbon, Seville.

She sensed all this. 'You mustn't be afraid. I'm not what you might think, you're not taking a streetwalker with you. I'm crazy, but that's something else. Every now and again I need money, or else I need to feel like a spendthrift, then I go out and do what I did today with you, next to some bus stop, or a news stand, or there might even be someone following me. But it's not my profession. It may happen two or three times a month, no more than that, though rather more often lately because I had to leave the job I was doing, and I can't live only on the arithmetic and geography lessons my sister gets for me, apart from the fact that the mothers of those dunces never pay. I'm a criminal to myself, but I'm the kind of girl you can introduce to anyone, my father is a teacher in Naples, I didn't want to tell you, but I have to give you my references, you won't want to take with you someone off the street, and I'm not like that. My sister works for the phone company, she got me a job there, too, but I can't stand it in those henhouses so I left. Then this thing happened, and I don't have any choice: either you take me with you, or tomorrow I end it all.'

'What thing happened?' Her words had rooted him to the spot.

'I'm sorry, darling, I can't tell you. You're a gentleman, that's obvious from the way you're dressed. I'm asking you what I ask you because I've seen that you're a gentleman, I wouldn't tell the kind of louts you find around here if I prefer milk or lemon with my tea.' Then she fell silent, giving him time to think.

And he thought. Despite all his sensitivity, he was deaf to the appeal of what could be defined as madness. Leaving for three months with a girl he had met only a few hours earlier, even he would call that madness, and in his world madness was in bad taste. But it depressed him, and he said, depressed, 'I can't.'

'Why can't you? Don't tell me it's because of the money.'

No, maybe not because of the money, although he didn't like spending his allowance and then having to resort to his father. 'Not only because of the money.'

Somehow, she could read his thoughts. 'I understand. You can't suddenly take off for three months, you have a family, maybe a girlfriend, you ought to tell your father, explain, make up some story: nobody's ever free. I know all that, but all I can do is repeat the same thing. I'm not trying to blackmail you emotionally, you're the dearest, most polite, most sensitive man I've ever met. But only you can save me. If you don't, the only other thing I can do is slit my wrists.'

'Why me?' Her last words had made him tense: they sounded like a threat.

'Because I don't have anyone else. There's no other solution, no other remedy. Either you let me get in your car and take me at least a thousand kilometres from here or I'll do what I said.' Her voice was normal, without emphasis, without drama: she was simply explaining, as if to one of her pupils.

That was what struck him and started making him anxious. 'I ought at least to sort things out with my father, I can't be away for three months like that, there's my work, too . . . Maybe we can meet again in a couple of days, maybe I can manage to—'

'Darling, there's no time. And even if there was, you wouldn't come back. Either we go away now, immediately, and you let me stay away with you as long as possible, or there's no point.' She kept repeating the same grim dilemma. Then she fell silent again, leaving him more time to think.

But maybe he had stopped thinking. The anguish had made him nervous, and nervousness makes us closed and unemotional, it gives rise to cold thoughts. Maybe this was hysteria, lucid hysteria. A normal woman wouldn't just decide to kill herself one day and then ask the first man she meets to save her because she doesn't want to die and to take her away. This was abnormal behaviour, and the suspicion that he was dealing with someone abnormal sent a chill down his spine. He didn't know what else to say to her.

She waited, smoked, looked inside her handbag, looked at the marathon runners of the autostrada coming in and out of the bar, opened her handbag again, looked inside, then said, 'Please, let's go.'

They got back in the car. Davide drove in silence, not very fast, and at the first station he left the autostrada, drove the long way round through secondary roads and came back to the entrance to the autostrada, but on the other side, the lane that led back to Milan.

'No, no,' she began to moan. 'I don't want to go back to Milan, take me away, take me away.' Her childlike whining was completely unexpected in a woman like her, it was a sign of hysteria, he thought.

'I'll talk to my father tonight, maybe I can convince him and tomorrow we'll leave.' He was lying, the way a doctor lies to a seriously ill patient.

'No, if you leave me we'll never see each other again, take me away now.' She started moaning even more loudly as soon as he got in the lane to Milan.

'Calm down, I can't now, don't do that.'

'No, take me away immediately, otherwise I'll have to kill myself.' She was rigid, distant, hidden behind her hair, yet imploring.

'Please try and calm down, when we get to Milan we'll talk some more.' But now he was afraid, a woman having a crisis would make any man afraid, all he wanted now was to hold on until he could get rid of her without making a scene, but at any moment she might start screaming, struggling, forcing him to stop in the middle of the autostrada, the traffic police would arrive: hell and damnation, you spend five minutes with a woman, and after it you find yourself smashed to bits, as if you'd fallen from the last floor of the Pirelli skyscraper. The woman had seemed so calm, and now this was happening.

'Turn back, darling, take me away.' It was the same continuous lament, the obsessive lament of a little girl asking for ice cream, mummy ice cream, mummy ice cream, mummy ice cream, mummy ice cream.

He decided not to answer her any more.

'Take me away, for pity's sake, or I'll kill myself . . . Get out here, get out here, at this service station, turn back, take me away, for pity's sake . . . Take me away, darling, if only you knew, if only you knew you'd take me away immediately.'

Davide tried not to listen to her, if he listened to her he would yield, if only to make her stop. He tried to distract himself, but there were not many things to concentrate on in the landscape, unless you were a lover of pylons. In the rearview mirror he could still see that beautiful Mercedes 230, somewhere between coffee and bronze in colour, maybe he was wrong, but he had the feeling he had seen it behind them on the outward journey, too: he liked his Giulietta very much, but he'd have liked a Mercedes sports car like that one even more.

'No, no, no, I don't want to go back to Milan.'

He could talk to Signor Brambilla, who was in charge of the family finances, ask if he could get him a Mercedes like that without his father seeing the accounts and going crazy. They had almost reached the end of the autostrada.

'No, no, no, no, no, I'm going mad, turn back.' She took her handkerchief from her purse as he pulled up at the exit toll gate, and while he was paying, the ticket collector looked inside and saw her wiping her eyes: she looked ridiculous with her big sunglasses pulled forward and her hair covering her forehead. Davide heard a click, something must have fallen from the handbag, but the frenzy of that scene, the ticket collector's impassive, mocking look—"He took the girl for a ride, and on the way back she's causing trouble"— was too much for him.

'No, no, no, turn back, no, no, no, take me away.'

He braked abruptly, throwing everything to the right, almost into the fields. Around them, against a sky red with sunset, the buildings of Metanopoli burned dully, and that *no, no, no, no* was shredding his nerves, for the second time in his life—the first had been as a soldier when he had hit the fellow in the next bunk—he raised his voice and roared, 'That's enough, get out, I can't stand it any more!'

Her moaning faded abruptly, like a radio when you take the plug out. Because of her large round sunglasses he could not see her eyes, but her half-open mouth told him how scared she was. For a moment she sat there, frozen, her mouth frozen, then she opened the door and got out, clumsy with terror, as if she thought he would hit her if she didn't get out, and no sooner was she out of the car than Davide closed the door behind her and drove off. He angrily overtook the Mercedes 230, which was now going at forty kilometres an hour: cars are always better than anything, better than any woman, you can drive a car twenty days in a row, but after only twenty minutes a woman becomes impossible.

He felt safe only when he got to the garage near his house, and slowly descended the ramp into the basement, which had become a science-fiction-like grand hotel for cars, with young men in aerodynamic costumes from Cape Kennedy and Marine caps, talking in broad Milanese phrases, all of which immediately re-established a more familiar climate.

He was a naturally tidy young man and before handing over the car always looked inside. So he immediately saw the handkerchief and that strange, tiny object, which was what he had heard falling from the girl's handbag as she dried her eyes. He put everything in his pocket, feeling embarrassed, because one of the Marines was waiting.

'Good evening, Signor Auseri.'

'Good evening.'

He crossed the Piazza Cavour, which was shady in the placid sunset. From the zoo came a vague smell of lions overheating. He went into the Galleria Cavour and stopped at the Milanese Bar, even here he was the only customer, surrounded by sweets, chocolates, pasta, bottles, and after the chilled beer the heat of his nervous anger faded inside him in a flash, and the thought came to him: 'And now she's killing herself.'

He left the bar, crossed the Piazza Cavour to the Via dell'Annunciata, and went up to his apartment. 'No, she isn't killing herself, she'll get over it.'

In the apartment there was nobody but the maid: his

father was in Rome, he spent more time in Rome than he did here.

He had a shower, and as the water crashed over him, he tried to calm down, and began to mutter. 'Women are mad, they really do kill themselves.'

He got dressed and went into the smaller reception room, part dining room, part library and part passage leading to the main living room of the apartment. 'But even if she does kill herself, what's that got to do with me?'

He had dinner at home, with the TV on: things were going badly in Vietnam, an American parachutist almost shot at him from the screen. 'I could at least have brought her back to the centre of town. Throwing her out like that in the middle of the fields in Metanopoli must have made her even more desperate.' On the screen now, a man was expounding all sides of the question in the matter of air pollution in winter, due to large factories and home heating: in the middle of summer, with the temperature at thirty-six degrees, the subject wasn't of much interest to him. What interested him much more, for a few moments, was the cone-shaped head of the new maid, a middle-aged lady who had asked him vaguely, with a vague smile on her face, for permission to sit down on the sofa and watch television, and now he was looking at her, her cone-shaped head covering a third of the screen, in the stuffy solitude of that apartment that no TV programme would ever break, perhaps nothing ever would, not even if they held a masked ball. 'If she kills herself and someone saw me with her, they'll summon me to Police Headquarters.'

He felt icily unhappy: he was always a little that way, on those evenings watching television with the maid, because in the morning he had to go to Montecatini, but that evening he was even more unhappy than usual. What if he went back to Metanopoli to have a look? He glanced at his watch, as if he could be so stupid: oh, yes, of course, the woman would still be there waiting for him, imagine that, and even if she was still there, worse still, she would start again, 'Take me away.' That was when he started to feel really bad.

All night, and all next day at the office, he felt bad. He read the *Corriere* headline by headline, but there was no news of any girl who had killed herself. There was nothing in *La Notte* or *Il Lombardo* either. In the evening the refined maid with the cone-shaped head was off, and he went and ate a couple of rolls in the Milanese Bar. Between one roll and another he crossed the street: the last edition of *La Notte* must be out by now. There were slim pickings these days for the afternoon papers: they couldn't always put the heatwave or the Chinese atomic bomb on the front page, so journalists, with ulcers or without, tried to make a big thing out of local news—the husband who had hit his wife with an iron and then thrown it out of the window, the couple caught committing obscene acts in a public place (the Idroscalo, even supposing you could do anything different at the Idroscalo anyway)—and that was how Davide saw all he had feared on the front page of one of the newspapers, a headline over five columns, GIRL SLASHES WRISTS IN METANOPOLI, which gave the news a touch of geographical drama, as if the fact that someone could slash their

wrists in Metanopoli was a pointer to future trends, a sign of
the times: these days you don't slash your wrists, boringly, in
your own home, or in old places and cities with old names,
Pavia, Livorno, Udine, today you slash your wrists in the
new centres of oil and heavy industry, a slave, even in this
last act of will or desperation, to the ruthless onward march
of progress.

With the newspaper in his hand Davide crossed the street
again and ate his second roll in the Milanese Bar, surrounded
by a half a dozen people having a drink before going to the
Cavour cinema to see a film whose female protagonist, judg-
ing at least from the photographs on display, was certainly a
very interesting case of mammary elephantiasis.

The reporter had made everything really dramatic,
describing how the grass in the field where the girl had been
found with her wrists slashed had turned blue: as far as he
was concerned the green of the grass combined with the red
of the blood gave blue. The cyclist Antonio Marangoni, who
wasn't a racer, but simply a seventy-seven-year-old, an early
riser who was on his way from his farmhouse to Metanopoli
by bicycle, had discovered the girl, now dead, and raised
the alarm. Next to the girl had been found a flat handbag,
almost like a large man's wallet, and inside it a letter for her
sister. The contents of the letter were not revealed, but the
reporter had heard from sources at Police Headquarters that
it was the usual request by someone killing themselves to
those remaining behind to forgive them. In brackets was a
note indicating that the item continued on page 2.

Davide went home to drink some whisky and read the

continuation on page 2. He read it several times, and each time he finished reading he got up and poured himself a whisky, taking the bottle from a cabinet that must have been a shoe cupboard in the nineteenth century.

She had said she would kill herself and she had killed herself. She had not even waited until the following day, she had cut her wrists as soon as he had thrown her out of the car, she had hidden in a bush, next to Antonio Marangoni's farmhouse, like a dying animal, and there she had finished dying, because she had already made her mind up, and had already written the letter begging her sister for forgiveness: she'd had it in her bag when she was with him by the river, the same bag where she had then put the money he had given her.

But she didn't want to die, she had to but she didn't want to, she had moaned all the way back, no, no, no, she didn't want to, and if he had taken her away, if they had gone far away, as she had kept asking him, she wouldn't have killed herself, she would still be alive. Night and day he remembered her large round sunglasses, and her imploring voice, the moaning, the whining. He had killed her, he kept thinking that as he leafed through the bright files in the bright folders on his desk at Montecatini, and gradually he discovered that by drinking a certain amount of whisky, any whisky, that feeling that he had a murderer inside him, the way a small gift box given at a wedding can contain a cyanide capsule, grew weaker. After even more whisky, it disappeared altogether.

6

As soon as Duca realised from Davide Auseri's story that the young man hadn't killed anyone, the desire to punch him made him grit his teeth as if he had an unbearable itch. Damned psychopaths, asthenics, schizophrenics! Then the young man's face, turned soft with anguish, like mayonnaise coming loose from a jar, aroused his pity.

'Let's go back to my sister's.' They had been sitting for almost an hour in the car, parked outside the Musocco cemetery and, what with the surroundings and the senseless story Davide had told him in a senseless monologue, he felt the need for a change of scenery. He didn't have many places to go with this would-be madman: not his apartment in the Via dell'Annunciata, no, the great Engineer Auseri might turn up at any moment, nor could they go back to the villa in the Brianza, maybe to a hotel, but later: for now he preferred to take him to his sister's. He telephoned her, from a bar, unexpected visitors are never welcome, while Davide drank freely at the counter. Let him drink.

'I'm coming back with my friend, the one you met before. You'll have to be patient, you're going to have to help me, can you get my room ready for him?'

'Has something happened?'

'No, nothing, just a crisis of imbecility.'

On the way there, he stopped at a pharmacy, bought a little tube of the most basic sleeping pills, and once they got to Lorenza's apartment he made Davide lie down on the bed and gave him a pill and, like a babysitter with a child, sat there watching him until he fell asleep, which happened almost immediately, because after his confession the neurotic giant was exhausted and fell into what was more a state of collapse than sleep.

Then he put Sara to bed, too—in his arms the little rascal fell asleep immediately—and when he and Lorenza were alone in the kitchen, which was shady although not cool, he told her that he almost felt like crying.

'If it was just a matter of weaning him off alcohol, it'd be an easy job, but the man has a guilt complex about a murder, he's been drowning his sorrows in whisky for a year without telling anybody. The idea that he killed a girl has been simmering inside him, and even Freud would take years to get it out of his head. As soon as he's alone he'll try to cut his wrists, the same method the girl used, and in the end he'll succeed.'

'You can tell his father, he can put him in a clinic, and you can look for an easier job.'

'Yes, I could do that. He's in a clinic, one month, two, six, whatever you like, and when he gets out he slits his wrists.' He finished eating the thick slice of cooked ham which Lorenza had made him for lunch. 'And then I'll be the one who's haunted by the thought that if I'd stayed with him I could have saved him. We're too sensitive. In other words we're ridiculously divided into two distinct categories, those with hearts of stone and the sensitive. One man can kill his own family, wife, mother, and children, then in prison calmly ask for a subscription to a puzzle magazine so that he can do the crosswords, while another man has to be admitted to the psychiatric ward because he left the window open and his little cat climbed up on the windowsill and fell from the fifth floor: he thinks he killed his cat, so he goes mad.'

At about seven in the evening Davide Auseri woke up, soaked in sweat: he had all the characteristics of an old maid affected by hypothyroidism, even the nervous sweats. Duca made him take a cold bath, staying with him in the bathroom because he didn't feel confident leaving him alone, while Lorenza ironed Davide's suit and shirt and forced him to eat half a roast chicken that she had gone to buy from the nearby butcher. Duca twice filled his glass with red wine, then asked him to come into his study. There had been no conversation: it was as if Davide had closed his front door and had stopped receiving visitors. Duca would make him receive him, by force if need be.

'Sit down there,' he said. This was the study his father had made for him to use as a surgery: the display case with the medical samples was still there from three years earlier, the couch covered with plastic that looked like leather, the screen in front and in a corner by the window which looked out on the Piazza Leonardo da Vinci, the glass table with the penholder and the long drawer with the little cards in it, maybe more than a hundred—his filing cabinet. His father had imagined it would soon be full of the names of all the sick men, women, and children who turned to him to be cured. What an imagination! He lowered the Anglepoise and lit a cigarette.

'I don't know if you've noticed, but I haven't even tried to tell you that you didn't kill anyone, and that you're not to blame for that girl's death.' He stood up and went in search of something to use as an ashtray, came back with a little glass bowl, and sat down again. 'And I'm not going to try now. If you want to think of yourself as a murderer, go ahead. There are people who think they're Hitler, and you're suffering from the same disease. I'm telling you that right now, before I hand you back to your father, because I can help a young man who drinks a little, but I can't do anything for someone who's mentally ill.'

He hadn't expected it but at that first knock, the door opened immediately. 'If I'd taken her with me she wouldn't have killed herself, it isn't a mental illness, it wouldn't have taken any effort, on the contrary, I'd have liked it, I could have taken her away with me, I wouldn't even have had to say anything to my father, I could have phoned Signor Brambilla and asked him to tell my father that I was taking a short holiday, my father didn't even care all that much whether or not I worked for Montecatini, it was only to give me something to do, I'd only have had to take her with me for a few days, until the crisis had passed.' He was panting as he spoke, but it wasn't because of the heat: the idea of being considered mentally ill, and by a doctor to boot, had shaken him.

'Oh, no, Signor Auseri,' Duca interrupted him, 'it's pointless for you to try and drag me into this discussion,' his tone was cool and mocking, 'in the treatises on psychiatry there are famous examples of absurd dialectic. I have no desire to have it demonstrated by you that you killed that girl. By the same reasoning, the gas company is responsible for all the people who gas themselves to death, and if you were the director of the company, you'd start drinking whisky and wanting to die. So forget it, the more you persist with this idea, the more you demonstrate how serious your case is.' That must have touched a sore point, because he saw Davide raise his fist, as if about to pound on the table, but he didn't, he simply held it like that, in mid-air.

'But if I had taken her with me . . .' He was almost crying.

'Enough!' Duca now pounded on the desk with his hand. 'A normal person doesn't bother with ifs. But you're not normal. Here's more proof: for a year, your father did everything he could to find out why you'd started drinking like that, why you were behaving so strangely, he nearly broke your jaw with a poker, so why didn't you ever tell him the truth? What were you afraid of?'

The reply came, unexpected and limpid. 'Because he wouldn't have understood.'

He was right, Engineer Auseri wouldn't have understood: depth psychology isn't something emperors wish to engage with. Of course he didn't tell him he was right. 'Okay. In that case why did you tell *me* the truth? You've known me less than twenty-four hours, and I never even asked you.' He already knew why but he wanted to see if Davide was capable of explaining it.

'I hadn't been back to the Via dei Giardini for almost a year,' he said, looking down at the floor, 'and this morning you took me there, you parked your car almost at the same spot where I had parked it a year ago, and you left me there while you went into Police Headquarters . . . And then you took me to the cemetery, you talked to me about your father, I saw all those graves . . .'

Exactly: without knowing it, that morning he had put young Auseri in a position to unblock his complex, and now, in order to unblock that other, more dangerous, complex— guilt—he had managed to scare him into thinking he might be mad, and poor Michelangelo-esque Davide was trying to demonstrate to him that he wasn't: thinking you're mad is more painful than thinking you're guilty of murder. But it was too unpleasant a job: selling pharmaceuticals would have been less lucrative but also less disagreeable.

'That handkerchief and that other object she left in the car,' Davide resumed, 'I didn't want to see them, they made me feel bad, but I couldn't resist, I'd take them out, I'd think about when she wiped her lips and instead of taking her with me I threw her out . . .'

He was a pitiful spectacle, so athletic and yet so morbidly sensitive, but at least he wasn't closed up in himself as if inside a ball of concrete, the way he had been before.

'All right, I'd like to see those things for myself. Where are they?' Just to allow him to let off steam as much as possible, to get him to free himself, at least a little. Davide didn't want to tell him at first, but he insisted.

They were in his beautiful soft suitcase, in an internal pocket with a zip.

'I'd have liked to throw them away and never see them again, but even thinking about where I'd throw that made me feel bad.'

Of course, the morbid psychology of memories. On the glass surface of the little table, he now had the famous handkerchief which, in Davide's mind, was the handkerchief of the girl he'd killed, and that little object, which looked like a tiny telephone receiver for a doll, two little wheels joined on one side by a strip of metal, no more than three centimetres in length. He barely looked at the handkerchief, but picked up this other object and held it in the palm of his hand. In a tone very different from his previous sharp, harsh one, he asked, 'This object fell out of the girl's handbag that day, is that right?'

'Yes.'

'Do you know what it is?'

'No. I thought it might be a sample of some kind of beauty product, but I don't know.'

'Have you tried to open it?'

'I never even thought it could be opened.'

'But you just said you thought it was a sample. A sample can be opened.'

'I never thought too much about it. Just looking at it makes me feel bad.'

He understood. 'I'll tell you what it is: it's a Minox cartridge.' He saw that Davide didn't know what a Minox cartridge was, so he explained it to him. 'Inside here is a strip of film about fifty centimetres long and less than a centimetre wide, on which you can take more than fifty photographs with a miniature camera called a Minox.' And having finished the explanation he forgot him, as if he no longer had him there in front of him, as if Davide didn't exist and he was alone, in the air sickly with heat, in the soft, antiquated light of that lamp, a professional's lamp, as the shop assistant had said to his father when he bought it for him. Only him and that cartridge.

A Minox wasn't exactly a camera for amateurs. Little larger than a cigarette lighter, it had been used by spies during the war to photograph documents, as any reader of espionage novels knew. It could take photographs in fog and through smoke, which was why it had also been used a lot by war correspondents. But it required practice to take photographs with such a small camera, it wasn't easy to frame the shots or keep the camera still. For an amateur, taking fifty photos with a single cartridge was too much, but for a professional it was ideal. And being so small, the film could easily be sent by post, and equally easily be hidden. He had once read a novel in which a spy had kept a Minox cartridge in his mouth when crossing a border and still managed to speak, though that could, of course, have been an exaggeration on the part of the writer—or maybe the character had a larger than average mouth.

He still felt nervous. He didn't like pointless, infantile fantasies, but this cartridge came from a woman's handbag and there weren't many women so keen on photography that they'd use a Minox. Besides, the girl wasn't exactly a normal, home-loving individual: every now and again she went out, let herself be picked up by a man and went with him, for financial reward. Superintendent Carrua would have defined such behaviour as prostitution, which might not have been very chivalrous, but was certainly accurate. In addition, this girl, for reasons she had not wanted to reveal, had intended to kill herself, and in fact had killed herself. He didn't want to speculate, but he would have liked to know if this film had been exposed completely or partly—it must have been through a camera because there wasn't a strip of film between the two spools, as there would have been if it hadn't been used—if after a year it could still provide a sufficiently clear negative and, above all, what had been photographed. Of one thing he was sure: that these wouldn't be holiday snaps, an old lady under a beach umbrella, a woman bathing on the rocks, a group of friends on a beach playing with a large ball.

And all these things he wanted to know immediately, he wouldn't sleep or eat or think about anything else until he did.

He wrapped the cartridge in the handkerchief and put it in his pocket. 'Excuse me a moment, I'll be right back.' The telephone was in the hall. The kitchen door was ajar and through it he could see Lorenza knitting a winter outfit for Sara and listening to the radio. He smiled at her and gestured to her to remain seated, he didn't need anything. He looked at his watch: nine o'clock.

'Superintendent Carrua, please.'

'Who shall I say is calling?'

'Duca Lamberti.'

A long wait, a few clicks, then Carrua's voice, a little distorted. 'Sorry, I'm yawning.'

'I'm sorry, too, but I needed to talk to you urgently.'

'You could have come here without phoning, I'm always ready to see you.'

'I wanted to know if the photographic lab was open.'

'The lab? Obviously it's closed. They're still doing a short week.'

'I'm sorry, I didn't want to wait until tomorrow morning.' He couldn't, he'd rather go and rouse some photographer from his bed.

'If it's urgent, I could have it opened and get hold of the technicians.'

'It *is* urgent. I'll explain when I get there.'

'All right, I'll be waiting.'

'I'll be bringing Auseri's son with me.'

Ten minutes later, he and Davide were in the Via Fate-benefratelli, and by 11:40 Carrua's large desk was covered in photographs in 18×24 format: the enlargements from the Minox film. There were also two large bottles of Coca-Cola on the desk. Only Davide had not taken his jacket off: they had sat him down at the far end of the room, in front of the table where the typewriter was, and there he had stayed and there he was even now, while they looked at the photographs.

'What are you thinking, Duca?'

'I'm sorting the photographs.'

From a puritan point of view, they were obscene images. They were extremely clear, in spite of being enlarged, and technically excellent. Against a vague background of clouds, the kind you found in old photographic studios, stood the subject, a naked woman.

'There isn't much to sort: half are of the brunette and half of the blonde.'

That was true: there were about twenty-five photographs

of the same dark-haired girl, and twenty-five or twenty-six of the blonde. It could have been claimed that these were artistic images, however daring, in fact the poses seemed to have a modicum of aspiration towards artistry, but that would have been splitting hairs. The poses of the two girls were openly alluring, it wasn't just their nakedness, it was also the gestures of the arms, the position of the legs. In most of the photographs the girls were hiding their faces, but not in all of them. They couldn't have been more than twenty-two or twenty-three years old.

'Where did you put the Radelli girl's file?' he asked Carrua.

'Oh yes, it's in the drawer.' Carrua gave it to him.

It was a large yellow folder, quite creased, the dossier on the suicide of Alberta Radelli. It contained her photograph, the death certificate issued by the pathologist, a photostat of the letter the girl had written to her sister asking forgiveness for killing herself, an officer's report, an overall report made by the appropriate office, three or four pages summarising the interviews conducted with a number of people: the suicide's sister, the famous cyclist Antonio Marangoni, the caretaker of the building where the dead girl lived with her sister. There were stamps, signatures, words underlined in red, and large blue seals. Duca extracted the photograph of the girl, taken from her licence, and showed it to Carrua along with one of the photographs from the Minox.

'It could be,' Carrua said.

'We can soon find out. Davide, come here a moment, please.' Davide Auseri at last stirred himself and came towards Duca, who showed him the photographs from the Minox, those of the brunette and those of the blonde, but not the photo taken from the licence. 'Is there anyone you know here?'

It was a nice office, large and quiet, a good place to work at night. Carrua had an apartment somewhere in the city, but even he might not have been entirely sure where it was, he only went there when he remembered the address and wanted to take a bath, but the rest of the time he preferred to sleep in the little room next to the office on the divan bed, with piles of newspapers and press releases on the floor, along with the telephone. His real home was in Sardinia, where he had been born, but he couldn't get there more than once a year, for a few days. His other real home was this one here, his office, which was always full of things and people. Now there was this young man, looking at these photographs. Carrua was not a particularly sensitive man, but he felt sorry all the same to see Davide's face as he looked at the photograph of the brunette.

'That's her,' Davide said.

'You mean this girl is the same one who was found in Metanopoli a year ago?' Duca asked.

'Yes.'

'What about the other one, the blonde? Do you know her?'

'No.'

Duca turned to Carrua. 'Can you send for a bottle of whisky?' he said, adding, 'I'll pay.' He took Davide by the arm and walked him over to the window.

'Stay there for a moment, the whisky will be here soon.' He moved a chair close to him, as if he was an old man. 'As soon as you don't feel like standing, sit down.'

'What brand?' Carrua asked.

'The most expensive,' Duca said.

A half glass of whisky gave Davide's eyes a less remote expression. 'Don't be afraid. That shivering inside will soon pass. Drink some more.'

He drank, too, quite a bit. He might end up weaning the young man off drink, but becoming an alcoholic himself. 'And now let's analyse these photos.' He sat down next to Carrua. In prison you lose your own personality, he realised, you lose warmth, you become frozen, and that was why he had to drink. 'These photographs were taken by a professional in a studio. Technically they're perfect, aesthetically a little less so. The photographer hasn't bothered much with the arrangement of the subject, all he's interested in is the shutter, the speed, the light. My second observation is how strange it is to do studio photographs, and photographs of this kind, with a Minox. A Rollei or a Contax would have been better, or the usual plate cameras you get in studios. To obtain these photographs, they must have placed the Minox on a tripod, and it's quite a problem, attaching it to a tripod, you need special nuts and bolts that aren't easy to get hold of, because people don't usually need to place a camera weighing fifty grams or a little more on a tripod that weighs fifteen kilos.'

'When did you study photography?' Carrua said.

'I never studied it, I'm only a layman, but I had a friend

who was a photographer.' He looked at Davide, who had sat down and was looking out of the window, with his back to them. 'My third observation is that the girls are not professional prostitutes used to this kind of work. Look at the poses: as far as looking sexy goes, they don't know much, especially the blonde. The brunette's a little better, she has a little more class, but she's innocent. The blonde, on the other hand, is either very vulgar, or just clumsy.'

Carrua was looking through a dozen photographs as he spoke. 'A very precise analysis.'

'The last thing is what you have to think about: What was the purpose of taking more than fifty photographs of this kind? That's your job. But there's something even more problematic, or at least something I think is serious.' He picked up the yellow file again and took out the few sheets of paper it contained. 'When a girl lies down in a field and slits her wrists, she has to use something sharp to do it with. Then she can do one of two things: if she has a lot of self-control and is very tidy, she puts the sharp object back in her purse, if she's already in a state of shock, she abandons it, she drops it near her, or else keeps it in her hand. But the officer's report doesn't mention any sharp object found near the body. Nor was any such object found in the girl's purse. It's unlikely that the girl would slit her wrists with the first sharp thing she finds in the field where she's hidden herself, for example the lid of a tin can, a thorn, a fragment of glass, but even if we admit that, the pathologist's report contradicts it: the cuts to the veins are straight and clean. You can't make a cut like that with a tin can or a piece of glass.'

Carrua looked through the papers in the file. 'Here it is: ". . . complete list of what was found in the place where the body of the above-mentioned Alberta Radelli was discovered . . ." It seems they searched, but didn't find anything sharp. If it was a small blade it might have got lost in a field.'

They exchanged glances. They knew each other well and couldn't fool each other. 'You can't slander the Metanopoli police like that,' Duca said. 'If there'd been something sharp there, even within a radius of thirty metres they would have found it and put it on the list. You don't have a very high opinion of your fellow officers.'

'Your father always said that, it offended him.'

They both smiled, wickedly. And then Carrua said, 'I think you have something else to say.'

'Yes,' he said, 'the contents of the purse.' He looked towards the window. Davide was there, his back turned. 'Davide, no need to get up, just tell me how much money you gave the girl that day. Think carefully. Tell us what denominations it was in.'

Davide turned. Compassionately, the whisky had put to sleep the vipers that were poisoning him from inside. 'Let's see . . . They were ten-thousand-lire notes . . .'

'How many?'

'Let's see . . . I think two, yes, two, when we were in the Corso Lodi, because she didn't want to come, she was afraid . . . Then, by the river, she said she needed fifty thousand lire, and so I gave her another three notes of ten thousand . . . In my wallet I only keep notes of . . .' He suddenly broke off, and slowly turned back to the window.

'So,' Duca said to Carrua, 'when Davide left the girl she had fifty thousand lire in her purse, at least fifty thousand. Now I'll read you from the list how much there was by the time the police arrived: one ten-thousand-lire note, one thousand-lire note, three hundred-lire coins, two twenty-lire coins, four five-lire coins. If we assume the girl already had the small change before she met Davide, in other words, one thousand three hundred and sixty lire, and that the ten-thousand lire note was one of the five that Davide gave her, there are forty thousand lire missing.'

It was obvious, but Carrua checked the dog-eared sheet of paper all the same. 'Give me the pathologist's statement.' He read it carefully. 'It says here she can't have slit her wrists before eight o'clock, but probably after eight thirty.'

Duca looked again towards the window, almost sadly. 'Davide, don't get up: What time was it when you left the girl that day?' He saw immediately that the young man hadn't understood, he was dazed, but not with whisky. In Metanopoli, when you told the girl to get out of the car, what time was it, more or less?'

Davide didn't say, 'Let's see.' He said, 'The sun had set.'

'Could you still see?'

'Yes. The sun had only just set.'

'Given the season, it must have been seven or a little later,' Duca said to Carrua. 'The girl walked around for more than an hour before making up her mind, and in the meantime she could have spent forty thousand lire. Where and how I can't imagine, because Metanopoli isn't bursting with shops like the Via Montenapoleone.'

'She may have given them to someone,' Carrua said, 'or someone may have taken them, that's what you're trying to say.'

They didn't understand. Not even your closest and dearest friends always understand you. 'I'm not trying to say anything. Apart from one thing: that I can't deal with this young man. I don't like problems any more, and this is one big problem. Don't tell me you found me a good job and I don't want to do it, you have to realise that I can't afford to get mixed up in anything like this, it'd ruin me. After already being sentenced for homicide with extenuating circumstances, all I need is to be suspected of having links with the world of call girls and orgies and I'd really be messed up.'

'You're right,' Carrua said gently.

'I just wanted to show you that it isn't bad will,' Duca said. 'This business is for you now.'

'I'll get right on it.' Carrua picked up the phone. 'Send me Mascaranti.'

'I'm going to look for another job,' Duca said. 'Please get hold of Engineer Auseri, tell him whatever you want and give him back his son. Tell him he's not to be left alone.' He looked towards the window. 'I'm so sorry, Davide.'

Davide got up slowly, laboriously, even the small amount of air coming in through the window seemed to make him sway, and came towards them. 'Signor Lamberti,' he said.

They waited for what was coming next, they had to wait almost a minute.

'Don't leave me.'

They waited some more, he seemed still to have a lot of things to say.

'Don't leave me.'

He took another short step forward. 'Signor Lamberti.' He was an intelligent young man, he paid attention, he didn't need to be told things twice, he had grasped that Duca didn't like being called Dr. Lamberti.

There was nothing else to do but wait for him to speak, and they waited. They both knew now what he would say. And in fact he did.

'Don't leave me.'

He was repeating, without realising it, the scene the girl had played with him that day in the car. 'No, no, no, take me away with you, take me away.' He had even tried to cut his wrists, like her, and he would try again, as soon as he was alone. It was a kind of unconscious identification, a way of expiating his guilt.

Duca stood up, took him by the arm to support him, even though Davide was not drunk, walked him back towards the window, and made him sit down. 'You'll be all right, Davide.'

'Don't leave me.'

'Where's Mascaranti?' Carrua was screaming into the phone. 'Can I have the honour, or am I asking too much?'

'It's all right, I'm not leaving you.'

'If you leave me, it's over, I know what I'll do.'

Duca also knew what he would do, just as he had known when Signora Maldrigati told him she couldn't bear to live like that any more.

'I won't leave you.'

'Is he coming up?' Carrua yelled. 'Is my office on K2 or what? Why isn't he here yet?'

'It's all right.' He couldn't leave him. He was a specialist in socially redeeming work: euthanasia, saving troubled young people. He went back to Carrua's desk just as Mascaranti came in.

'I'm sorry,' Mascaranti said, 'I just finished my shift and went to have a beer.'

Even though he was short and dark, even though he still had his Sicilian accent, he didn't look like a policeman, more like a sportsman, a boxer, a racing cyclist, because of his athletic chest and huge hairy hands, and his trousers, even though they were not narrow, adhered to his legs almost like socks.

'We're not in the FBI here,' Carrua shouted, 'we're in Milan police Headquarters: when you've finished your shift you stay here.' He handed him the yellow file. 'See if you remember this case, that's your seal on the reports.'

In those hands, the sheets of paper were like butterflies in a dragon's paws. Mascaranti studied them for a while, without saying anything.

'He's forgotten how to read,' Carrua said nervously.

'Yes, I remember it,' Mascaranti said. 'The girl who slit her wrists in Metanopoli. I checked the reports from the Metanopoli police, I even showed them to you. Is something wrong?'

'Yes, something's wrong, even though I saw them and you saw them and the secretary general of the United Nations probably saw them.' Carrua did occasionally lower his voice, but it never lasted for long. 'What's wrong is that we don't know what the girl used to slit her wrists. Plus, she should have had more than fifty thousand lire in her purse and there was just over ten thousand when she was found.'

Duca rose to Mascaranti's defence. 'Nobody could have known that, apart from Davide who gave her the money.'

'And then there are these photos, which have just been developed after a year,' Carrua said. 'The brunette is the dead girl. Given the kind of photographs these are, there seems to be food for thought here.'

'There's also something else,' Duca said, his eyes still on Davide, 'anybody who wants to kill themselves by slitting their wrists does it at home, or in a hotel room, either in the bath, or in bed. It's a little unusual to hide in a field to do something like that, especially when you have a home to go to.'

'Didn't you think about these things when you signed the report?' Carrua screamed.

Mascaranti had long been immune to Carrua's shouting and screaming. 'Yes,' he said calmly, 'I thought about them, I even asked the pathologist if he thought it was worth doing a post-mortem. He told me he could do one if I wanted, but that his certificate was clear enough.' He read some phrases: ' ". . . Loss of blood . . . No other wounds, contusions or marks on the body." '

'Yes, I read that, too,' Carrua said, 'but I think we have to start again from the beginning. Take the file, and tomorrow morning go back to Metanopoli, question again everyone who was questioned before. And above all look into these pornographic pictures. I'll give you all the details tomorrow morning.'

'How did we get hold of these photos?' Mascaranti asked.

'I'll tell you tomorrow morning!' Carrua exploded. He didn't want to talk about Davide now. 'All right,' he said to Duca. 'Take our friend home. Tomorrow I'll contact Auseri and he'll come and collect his son, and you'll be free.' Duca said nothing, he was looking at the hard-faced Mascaranti, who had taken the yellow file and was clutching it to his chest.

'I'm talking to you,' Carrua said.

'Sorry.' Duca looked at him. 'I may have changed my mind.' It wasn't a real change of mind, he was just making yet another of his mistakes.

Carrua put the two empty bottles of Coca-Cola down on the floor. 'Go now,' he said to Mascaranti, 'and I'll see you tomorrow morning at ten.' He had already understood.

'I'm staying with Davide,' Duca said to Carrua, as soon as Mascaranti had gone out.

'If you want to,' Carrua said nervously: when his sensitivity was touched he became nervous.

'I do want to. Plus, I'd like to ask a favour.'

'Go on.'

'I want to be with Mascaranti on the investigation.'

Carrua was looking at the bottle of whisky. 'Give me a drop of that stuff.' He barely moistened his lips, just stared into the glass. 'Let me see if I've got this right, Duca, you want to investigate alongside Mascaranti.' It wasn't even a question.

'Something like that. I won't take an active part, but I'll be with Mascaranti.'

'First you wanted to drop everything, now you want to play cops and robbers.'

'I changed my mind.'

'Why?'

He didn't reply, and Carrua didn't insist, because he knew why. Davide was still there next to the window, straight, statuesque, devastated.

'All right. Tomorrow I'll send you Mascaranti.' Carrua covered the two lots of photographs, putting one photograph face down on each pile. It felt strange, looking at naked photographs of a dead woman. 'Where will you be?'

'I think it's best if we stay at the Hotel Cavour, that way we'll be nearby.'

'Yes, it's practical.' Carrua looked at his watch. 'I don't know how good you are as a policeman, so let me give you a test. Where would you start?'

He didn't reply this time either. Nor did Carrua insist this time, because he knew perfectly well where he needed to start: with Davide Auseri. Homicide disguised as suicide was something lots of people tried, almost always in vain, but even if the girl really had killed herself, Davide Auseri had been the last person to see her alive, and his story was just his story, and it might not necessarily be the truth, or at least not the whole truth. But neither of them had the stomach to pump him at the moment, neither he nor Carrua. They were even afraid of what might come out if they pumped him, or maybe not afraid, they felt pity, they felt sorry for him, both of them, he and Carrua. One day, before too long, they would have to ask Davide where he had been that evening, from seven until ten, and if he could tell them the name of someone who had seen him during those hours, and if he couldn't be clear about that, and if they suspected that the suicide of Alberta Radelli wasn't a suicide but that she had been murdered, then they needed him, Davide, to explain, as best he could, what was behind the girl's death, and what was behind those photographs, because whatever it was it wasn't anything good.

'I know what you're thinking,' Carrua said. 'I remember somebody doing that in 1959. A man whose wife always took sleeping pills at night. One night he gave her one more than usual, then slit her wrists and came to us in the morning to say he'd found her dead.'

'And how did you find him out?'

'We beat it out of him. It was Mascaranti who questioned him. When you think up a trick like that, you never think you might be beaten. There's no need of any Chinese torture, after the fifth or sixth slap from Mascaranti, a person has to decide before his brain explodes.'

'I didn't say she was murdered,' Duca said, standing up. He hoped, with all his heart, with all the last spark of trust in his fellow men, with all his anger, that it wasn't anything as nasty as that. He went to Davide. 'Come on, let's pitch our tents at the Cavour.' He put his hand on his shoulder and gave it a little fraternal squeeze.

PART TWO

*Every time we find a pimp we have to crush him . . . But what
exactly do you want to crush, my darling? The more of them you
crush, the more there are. And that's all right, but
maybe you have to crush them all the same.*

1

No, not everything was so nasty.

Davide had stayed in the car, behind the wheel. Mascaranti and Duca climbed to the third floor; as usual in this kind of building the lift was out of order, and on every landing you could hear at least one TV set with Milva singing on the Milva Club, and often even two. Milva was singing on the third floor, too, but the volume faded almost to nothing after they had rung the bell, then the door opened and the sister of the suicide or murder victim or whatever she was, the sister of Alberta Radelli, smiled shyly at Mascaranti.

'Police. We need to talk to you.'

She made the usual face that honest Italians make when they see a policeman, a pensive face that gradually turns increasingly anxious. She must have done something wrong, she couldn't remember what, but they had already found her out. The police had already been there, the year before, about poor Alberta, so what could have happened now? If she had been an American she would have replied, 'How can I help you?' in a polite, concerned tone, but she was an Italian from the South who the year before had been on the verge of losing her job with the phone company because her sister had killed herself and had been in the newspapers, so she didn't say anything, not even 'Yes,' just let them in, ran awkwardly across the little room to switch off the television set, blotting out Milva completely, and turned to look at them: one rather tall, rather thin, rather unpleasant-looking—that was him, Duca—the other short and stocky, and even more unpleasant-looking, and she didn't even ask them to sit down, just as she didn't tell them that it was illegal for the police to enter a citizen's home after sunset, because she didn't know the law, not that anyone did know it, and even if she had known it she still wouldn't have said anything.

'Is this your sister?' From a small leather briefcase Duca had taken out an 18×24 photograph and held it up to her, in the little room illuminated now only by a lamp with a plastic shade, bought at Upim or La Standa, and placed next to the TV set.

Every now and again his father had talked to him about his work and each time he did he told him, talking about his days in Sicily with the Mafia, that the only method which had proved effective over the years, with both criminals and honest people, with good and bad people, was a fist in the face. *These people are crafty, don't waste your time on them. Forensics is one thing and that's fine, but a police force using nice words, persuasion, psychological games, only makes new criminals. First give them a punch in the face, and then ask the question, you'll see, a person who's taken a punch responds better because he's realised that when the need arises you can talk his language. And if the person who's taken the punch is an honest man, don't worry, even honest men can have accidents.*

He had never liked the theory, and was even convinced that it was wrong, but now he had applied it. The photograph he had chosen to show the woman was one of the most indecent shots of her dead sister. It was just like a punch in the face.

Apart from looking at the photo, Alessandra Radelli did nothing, she didn't turn red, didn't turn white, didn't start to cry, didn't even say 'oh.' Nothing. But her face seemed to become smaller.

'Is this your sister?' he asked again, more loudly.

'Yes,' she said.

'Sit down, signorina.' He already knew everything about her, from the phone company where she worked, from the landlord—she paid her rent regularly—and from the caretaker—she never received men, nor had she received them when her sister was still there.

'Do you know anything about these photographs?'

She shook her head, she was starting to breathe heavily, it was probably the heat, the room was small, even more hot air came in from the window that looked out on the courtyard. Mascaranti had found the light switch and lit the thing which hung from the ceiling of the room and which revealed itself to be an attempt at a chandelier.

'What did your sister live on? Did she have a job?'

She knew perfectly well what they meant, and she started speaking. She seemed almost calm, but her face remained, inexplicably, smaller than when they had arrived. Of course, of course, Alberta had found work immediately, as soon as she had arrived from Naples: she had become a shop assistant.

'Where?'

She told them where, a shop, although the term was a little vulgar: better to say a 'men's boutique' in the Via Croce Rossa, where a young man enters, climbs a small carpeted staircase, and in a softly furnished little room his measurements are taken for a shirt by two young female shop assistants, or if he needs gloves for the car, French ties from Carven, original American pants, or anything else, the two shop assistants, guided by another lady, are always there, and one of the two assistants had been Alberta Radelli.

'How long did she work there?'

'Two or three months,' she wasn't sure.

Mascaranti was writing everything down.

'And then?'

'She left.'

'Why?'

She couldn't remember, maybe Alberta had quarrelled with the manageress.

'And after that?'

One by one, she told them all the places where her sister had worked, those that she knew, including the phone company. Mascaranti wrote them all down and then counted them up: in the year and a half she had been in Milan, Alberta Radelli had worked a total of almost eleven months, most of the time as a shop assistant. More than they had expected. The remaining seven months were taken up with intervals of unemployment.

'But she also gave lessons, I got a lot of lessons for her.' The famous arithmetic, history, and geography lessons to schoolboys.

'How much did she charge per lesson?'

'Six hundred lire.'

As much as an hourly cleaner but, apart from the social injustice and the debasement of cultural values, Alberta Radelli didn't have much to play with from these lessons. Cruelly, he turned over the photograph, which for a while he had kept face down, and showed it to her again. 'You realise your sister was doing something that wasn't very nice'—look at the photo, he seemed to be saying—'and I can't believe you didn't know anything about it, given that you lived together.'

She nodded, as if to say, yes, she knew something, and Mascaranti was getting ready to write it down, but all she said was that she had occasionally had her suspicions, because sometimes, even when she wasn't working, her sister gave her twenty or thirty thousand lire to help her with her monthly bills.

'And where did she say the money came from?'

'Once she told me she was translating a book from French and that she had been given an advance.'

'And did you believe her?'

Pitifully, she shook her head. 'No.'

'Did you tell her you didn't believe her?'

She hadn't really told her she didn't believe her: she had tried to find out if she had someone, she thought in fact that she did have someone, a man who might not have been very young, quite a generous man, but she hadn't tried to find out more, otherwise she wouldn't have accepted the money. In her clumsy way, she was sincere.

'So you didn't know,' he had to be even more brutal, 'that she earned that money by picking up men, or being picked up by them, different ones each time.'

No, she didn't know, and finally she began to tremble a little, but without crying, her whole face was visibly trembling, and yet she wasn't crying. 'What's happened? She's been dead for a year, we've already suffered so much, my father and I, what are you looking for now?'

It wasn't easy to explain what they were looking for and he didn't even try, because he himself wasn't sure exactly what they were looking for, maybe the truth, if he didn't find the very idea of the truth laughable. What is the truth? Does it even exist?

'All right, you don't know anything about this,' he said, putting the photo back in the leather briefcase, 'but maybe you can tell us something else that could help us. Your sister must have had friends, acquaintances. Did you ever see any friend of your sister's? Did your sister ever talk to you about anyone?'

The trembling ceased gradually, resignedly, because it's useless to tremble or cry, what's the point of it? 'She always said she was going to see some friend or other, but I can't remember all of them and anyway she only ever mentioned first names.'

He made her tell him what she remembered, and Mascaranti wrote everything down. The friend she remembered most was the schoolteacher. 'She hadn't graduated yet, but

Alberta called her the schoolteacher. She came here to the house, once, to pick her up.'

He was interrogating: having been interrogated so many times by the prosecuting attorney at the trial, and also in prison, he was now the one asking the questions, and it was an interesting experience. 'So you don't remember the name, is that right, you only knew her as the schoolteacher?'

No, she said, she remembered the name, Livia Ussaro: she must have written it down in the little address book.

'Thank you,' he said, 'could I see this address book?'

She went into the hall, took it from the hook from which it was hanging next to the telephone and brought it in to him. Without looking at it, he put it in the briefcase together with the photograph. 'I'll bring it back in a few days.' Livia Ussaro didn't sound a very likely name, it might be a pseudonym: start looking for a woman called Livia Ussaro and you probably wouldn't find anything. And he was getting tired of Mascaranti holding that little notebook that vanished inside his big hands, that little Biro, and the fact that he was writing everything down.

'Do you remember any other friends?'

'She mentioned so many. She'd say, *I'm going to see Maurilia*, or else somebody would phone and say, *this is Luisa, is Alberta there?*'

Was she winding him round her little finger, or was it innocence in a pure state, a precipitate of innocence, obtainable only in a laboratory?

'I was also thinking of men friends,' he said, patient but already irritable.

'No, never men.'

Mascaranti ran his Biro through his hair: he wasn't trying to write on his head, but the woman had said 'never men' quite seriously, straight out, it had come from her heart, she wasn't trying to deceive anyone.

'The photograph I showed you suggests your sister may have had a number of male acquaintances. Whatever it was she did, she's dead now, and there's no point in your trying to cover it up, we'll find out in the end anyway. Men must have phoned your sister, maybe lots of them, and some may have given their names. Please tell me the truth.'

'No man ever phoned her,' she said immediately, and she seemed genuinely sorry that she couldn't help him.

She wasn't lying. 'It's possible,' Mascaranti said. 'Maybe she didn't let them phone here because she didn't want to make her sister suspicious.'

While they were about it, they committed another violation of her rights as a citizen and did a quick search of the apartment.

'Your sister must have left some personal objects here. We'd like to see them.'

Unaware that the constitution gave her the right to refuse, she took them to the one bedroom in the apartment. There were two small beds like the cots of four-year-old children who sleep with teddy bears clutched to their chests, and indeed, on the light wooden headboards, bears, dogs, butterflies, and snails with long horns had been painted. 'She slept here with me, I left her clothes in the wardrobe, and everything else she had is in that suitcase on top of the wardrobe.'

Mascaranti pulled down the suitcase, opened it, and was about to start writing down everything it contained, but Duca stopped him. 'Leave it, there's nothing here.' There were a large number of bras, knickers and suspenders, some hair clips, a hairdryer, a novel by Moravia, a fountain pen, and an opened packet of cigarettes: Alpha, rather a strong brand for a young woman.

'We've finished.' No, not everything was nasty. Alberta's unfortunate sister may have been weak and foolish, but she didn't know anything, she hadn't been part of anything that wasn't above board. But in the hall, before they left, he still asked, 'Did you ever figure out why your sister killed herself?'

She said no with the same expression on her face, and finally her eyes grew moist. 'I don't know, it was terrible when they called me to the morgue, I hoped it wasn't her. The evening before she'd talked about the two of us going on holiday together, she said she wanted to go a long way away, somewhere abroad. She was cheerful, and I told her off, I said we didn't have enough money to go abroad, the landlord had asked for the latest instalment, it was fifty thousand lire, but she wanted to go on holiday, as far away as possible, she said.'

So that was why, that day, she had told Davide, alongside the gentle river, that she needed fifty thousand lire, and he had given it to her: it was for the expenses, the caretaker, the lift that didn't work, the heating, which her sister had to pay. But why she had killed herself, if she *had* killed herself; nobody knew, the sister even less than anyone else. He was pleased, at least there was something here that wasn't nasty. He tried as best he could to apologise for his cruelty. 'I'm sorry, signorina, if we disturbed you at night, but you work all day and we couldn't come at any other time,' but his attempt at kindness had a disastrous effect: Alessandra Radelli started sobbing and as they began descending the staircase they heard her sobs until the door closed.

Downstairs, they got in the Giulietta, and Davide was still at the wheel, the unofficial driver of an unofficial police commando, and having crossed the city they got out at the Hotel Cavour, their headquarters, as they did every evening.

'A bottle of dry Frascati, not chilled,' he ordered as soon as they were in the two connecting rooms. They took off their jackets, apart from Davide, and loosened their ties, even Davide. They were in the second phase of the treatment: change of poison. Davide could drink all the wine he wanted, even a wine that had an imaginary similarity in taste to whisky, but never again a single drop of whisky, or any other strong liquor. For two days, Davide had been holding out quite well, only his silence was tending to get worse.

Mascaranti was a bureaucrat, he needed to write a report of the work they had done during the day, and a plan of what they would do the following day.

'The sister's a dead end,' he said. 'She didn't tell us anything we didn't already know.'

'Good,' Duca said. He liked the Frascati the way it was now, almost warm, maybe more than Davide did. 'For now, let's concentrate on the address book,' he took it from the briefcase and handed it over to Mascaranti. 'Phone all those

numbers and if anyone replies who had anything to do with
Alberta Radelli or knew her, make a note of it and we'll
go and see them. Apart from this one,' he took back the
book and opened it at the letter *U*, made a note of the
number and the address: Livia Ussaro. Ussaro like *hussar*. A
nice pseudonym: maybe she even wore a jacket with gold
braid. 'Go and rest, we'll start again tomorrow morning.'
He gave him back the book. 'Remember we have to give
it back as soon as possible.'

It wasn't yet ten, but the silence in the two rooms was
total, the penultimate noise had been that of Mascaranti
closing the door as he went out, and the last noise that of
the Frascati gurgling into the glass as Davide poured it. Now
there was nothing, Davide certainly wouldn't say a word, and
Duca didn't like silence. He went and opened the two windows: it might let in the heat, but also a bit of traffic noise
from the Piazza Cavour.

'Do you like playing the policeman?' Apart from the
general silence, there was also Davide's silence, which ended
up arousing the bizarre suspicion that he was alive only in
appearance, that he continued to move, eat and drink, but as
if by inertial force, being already dead.

He didn't smile, and he needed time to respond. 'But I'm
not doing anything.'

'You're driving the car, you're following us in our investigations, you're doing errands. In the police, a driver is an
important person.' It was no use, he didn't react, he didn't
accept either conversation or jokes: for all his goodwill,
the Frascati didn't sustain him like whisky. Duca continued

speaking, as if he was alone: 'I really like playing the policeman. My father didn't like the idea of me following in his footsteps, but he was wrong.' Of course, he couldn't be a policeman even now, less now than ever. Especially in a case like this one. Carrua had been quite clear about this: 'If you find something that isn't right, don't be afraid to come out with it, but do it discreetly, for two reasons, one is that you can't be involved officially, otherwise we'll all be in trouble, the other is that as soon as the press find out we're taking an interest in the case, they'll manufacture another Montesi affair. It has all the elements, at least in the wild imagination of some journalists. If it is a Montesi affair, if really big names are involved, if there's something rotten behind all this, then don't be afraid, as I said, but before making a fuss about it we need proof, otherwise the papers will have a field day, and it's all over. Discretion, that's the order of the day.'

Discretion. In other words, like looking for something in the dark. Alberta Radelli's sister he had been able to tackle officially: we're police, answer our questions. But with the others, he had to be careful: on what pretext, for example, could the police question this Livia Ussaro, a whole year after Alberta's death, without being indiscreet, without risking kicking up a fuss? He looked for a pretext, but couldn't find one that was sufficiently intelligent, and he didn't like stupid pretexts.

But his desire to see Livia Ussaro was growing in him minute by minute, exacerbated by the aristocratic solitude of these hotel rooms, where you have everything you need to be comfortable, all the refinements you almost never get in your own home, and all that's missing is what you find in even the poorest home, something you can't define and which may not even exist, but everybody feels it as if it did exist. In a hotel room you move in a different way from the way you do in your own home, you look at things in a different way, maybe you even think in a different way. And so he made up his mind: these evenings at the hotel, with Davide there but not really there thanks to the decreasing supply of alcohol, weighed heavily on him. 'At least we can have a nice talk over the phone,' he thought, or predicted, as if he could see into the future.

He got up and went and sat down on the bed, next to the bedside table, where the telephone was, and asked the switchboard operator to get him the number of Livia Ussaro, then put down the receiver and waited. He saw Davide's sad, anxious profile, and on the table the bottle of Frascati on a large silver tray, aesthetically wrapped in a fine napkin. It was actually quite late to be telephoning a private number, a person he didn't even know, and after a year Livia Ussaro might have moved, or died, or emigrated to Australia: things go so quickly these days, oh, yes.

'Could I speak to Livia please?' he said as soon as he heard a middle-aged woman's voice.

'Who shall I say is calling?'

'Duca,' he said, simply. Among friends that was how people spoke on the phone.

'Duca?' the woman said.

'That's right, Duca.' Silence. The woman had moved away from the phone, she hadn't sounded very convinced by his name: *Duca*, as in duke. She wasn't the only one, at school he had even got into punch-ups with his wittier classmates: 'So what's your big brother, then, a Grand Duke or an Archduke?' The reply was always: 'He's this'—in other words, a kick in the kneecap or on the shin. His father had taught him that.

'Hello?' It must be her, the voice was low but quite girlish.

'Livia?'

'Yes, this is she, but I'm sorry, I don't remember . . .'

It *was* her, she still existed, really existed. His desire to talk to Livia Ussaro was about to be satisfied. 'I'm the one who should apologise. You couldn't remember me because we've never met.'

'Please, could you tell me your name again?' There was such coolness and yet such energy in her voice.

'Of course, but it wouldn't mean anything to you. I wanted to talk to you about someone we both know.'

'Either tell me your name, or I'll hang up.'

What a world of obsessive bureaucrats, from Mascaranti, who wrote everything down, to this woman who needed to hear the four or five syllables commonly defined as a name, any name: he could easily tell her his name was Orazio Coclite and what difference would it make? 'My name is Duca Lamberti, though you don't know me. But we both knew someone in particular.'

She didn't let him finish this time either. 'Wait, I've heard that name before. Oh, yes, of course, you're one of my idols! I was very innocent in those days, I used to have a lot of idols, I don't have many left, but you're one, except that my memory . . .'

He looked at the tip of his shoes, the shoes, with his feet inside, were real entities, and he had to convince himself that he was really talking to a woman who was telling him that he was her idol. In what sense? For what reason?

'. . . Three years ago, in the courtroom I shouted, "No, no, no, no!" when the judge read out the sentence, they dragged me outside and held me in a room for two hours, asking me who I was and who I wasn't, and I kept saying: "It's shameful, shameful, shameful, they shouldn't have sentenced him to prison," and they'd answer, "Signorina, keep quiet, otherwise we'll put you inside for causing a breach of the peace," and I cried all the way home. I'd attended the whole trial, I'd told everybody they had to acquit you, that you weren't guilty of anything, that in fact they ought to give you a prize, I'd quarrelled with people in the corridor outside the courtroom.'

Of course, she was talking too much, but her warm, low tone of voice didn't have the same irritating effect on him as the shrill chatter of many women. And besides, she was saying things he would never have expected, things he could never have imagined anyone saying to him, not even his father or his sister had ever said anything like that. He was an idol. He had a fan. Probably the only one.

'And now I didn't even remember your name! I really feel ashamed, you can't imagine all the arguments I've had about euthanasia, everyone's against it, they have their principles, the principle of respect for life, the principle of putting on evening dress to go to La Scala.'

'I'm very grateful, Livia.'

'Oh, I'm sorry, I don't usually talk so much, only when I'm speaking to someone intelligent, so I'm happy I can talk to you—but I'm sure there must be a reason you phoned me.'

'Yes, I wanted to talk to you about someone you used to know: Alberta Radelli.' A sudden silence, at the other end. 'Not right away, obviously. One of these days, whenever you like.' The silence continued, but she was still there, he could sense her presence, although he couldn't even hear her breathing. 'It's very important to me, and you could be a great help.'

And finally her voice, so low, so warm, and at the same time, not bureaucratic, but something similar, professorial, yes, that was the word. 'There are a lot of subjects I don't like talking about, and Alberta is the one I like least. And like all the things I don't like, I want to do them immediately.'

'Now?'

'Immediately.'

'Where can we meet?'

'Here in the Via Plinio. There's a bar right near my apartment. I'm sure I'll recognise you: at the trial I looked at you for hours on end. How soon can you get here?'

'In ten minutes.'

Life is a well of marvels, there's everything in it: rags, diamonds, cut-throats, and Livia Ussaro. He put down the receiver, feeling slightly dazed, as if he had drunk too much Frascati, and in fact he now poured himself half a glass, he looked at Davide, who wasn't alive even though he appeared to be living, and had a moment of weakness.

'I have to go out now, but I'll be back soon. I know you're not feeling too good about the wine, I'll have them send up a bottle of whisky, to help you stand the solitude and the darkness.' He really felt quite sorry. 'Act like a man, Davide: the less you drink the better it'll be.' This concession was a mistake, from both a medical and a psychological point of view. But even this time he had to risk it, above all he didn't want Davide to drink on the sly during his absence. If he wanted to drink, he was free to do so, he had Duca's permission.

He went out. Now he would see what Livia Ussaro looked like. He couldn't imagine her somehow, his only idea was that she must be quite tall.

2

She was indeed tall. She stood waiting for him at the door of the bar and he was impressed by the fact that, as soon as he got out of the Giulietta, she came towards him, with that warmth in her walk and in her eyes, as if she was greeting an old and dear friend. Until ten minutes ago, he hadn't even known he had a friend like her in the world, let alone so near.

'We can talk quietly here, it's the only bar in the area without a TV or a jukebox, so there are almost no customers in the evening.'

Her hair was brown, or rather black, a definite, natural black. It was cut quite short, a bit shorter than the hair of men who wear it long, but a little less short than the men who have it a normal length and go to the barber once every two weeks. A woman with short hair: he liked long hair, but he had to admit it looked good on her.

'You said things to me that were very, very . . .' it would be stupid to say 'kind,' but what could he say, so he broke off.

'I said to you a hundredth of what I should have said to you years ago. But now you want to talk about Alberta, so let's talk about her.'

She was wearing a dark green dress he liked a lot: smooth, high-necked, sleeveless. She was tanned, but normally, she didn't look like a Papuan, nor was she pale like girls who never sunbathe. That green, that tan, that black hair, matched the place very well, because it was all in gold, the walls were covered in gold plastic, and so was the counter, and the round tables gleamed dimly like old gold.

'Two beers.' They were the only customers, after serving them even the barman disappeared. There was no air conditioning, but a big fan with wide wooden blades gave the place an exotic, colonial tone and probably made it cooler than air conditioning might have.

'Alberta killed herself a year ago. What do you want to know about a dead woman?' Like him, she liked getting straight to the point, and when he didn't reply immediately, she continued, 'I can imagine how you met her. One evening you were going to the cinema alone, you hadn't found any other way to spend the evening, you got there in time for the last show, you parked your car and looked around, still undecided whether or not to go in, and that was when you saw her, standing there, looking a bit self-conscious, near the entrance to the cinema. You must have thought she was just a normal girl who'd been stood up by her boyfriend, or else she was waiting for a girlfriend who hadn't shown up. Before resigning himself to going to the cinema alone, a man has to try everything. So you smiled at her and it came as a pleasant surprise when she smiled back, a bit. Then you approached her, said some kind, considerate, witty words, and the rest is predictable.'

'I never met Alberta Radelli.' With this girl, he couldn't hide.

She seemed to turn colder. 'On the phone you told me you knew her.'

'Indirectly. I've heard a lot about Alberta.' Yes, a lot.

'I don't like equivocation. I can't believe you'd indulge in it. Don't disappoint me. A doctor willing to perform an act of euthanasia can't be an equivocator. Why are you interested in Alberta? Tell me the truth, or I'll leave now.'

She was a little too Kantian: behind her words there were categorical imperatives and prolegomena to any future metaphysics that would be able to present itself as a science. But she had beaten him and he had to tell her the truth. Or rather, he did more: he had brought with him the little leather briefcase, and gently—they weren't images to be shown in public—he showed her Alberta's photographs.

Livia Ussaro looked at them. 'I told her not to.'

He thought he was intelligent, but he didn't understand. He waited.

'She told me there was someone who was offering her thirty thousand lire for a few photographs like this, and I told her not to. We almost quarrelled, that time. She told me it was less dirty being photographed like that than going with the first man she found. I told her that wasn't true. She didn't take any notice, and did this filthy job all the same.'

It was all starting to become clear. 'What about this other girl, do you know her?' He took the photograph of the blonde girl from the briefcase.

'Maurilia, I only know her first name, I think she works at La Rinascente.'

Even clearer. Mascaranti would easily find a Maurilia, either in La Rinascente, or in all of Italy, there couldn't be many Maurilias. 'And how did you meet Alberta?'

Livia Ussaro started laughing, without a sound, the

silence of the gold-covered bar was not disturbed, but her somewhat masculine face grew softer with the laughter. 'How I met her doesn't matter. It's what led up to it that's important.'

'Then tell me what led up to it.'

'Of course, that's all I want to do, we all want to open our hearts completely,' she continued laughing the same way, but a little less. 'I don't know if I'm going to disappoint you, but what led up to it is this.'

She ordered two more beers. In a way, she was happy.

'Ever since I was sixteen, I'd wanted to experiment with prostitution,' she said, she had stopped laughing, and that tone had returned, not bureaucratic, but professorial, she was expounding a theory, which was as good as any other, that much was obvious. 'It wasn't morbid curiosity. You may be able to tell from my physical type that I'm frigid. Not completely. The gynaecologist and the neurologist have established that when the physical and environmental conditions are right, I can be a perfectly normal woman. Unfortunately these conditions are difficult to produce, and in practice it's as if I was frigid. Some people who aren't very perceptive think I'm a lesbian, which I find quite amusing.'

He was finishing his second beer, he was still thirsty, or maybe it wasn't thirst, and he felt, yes, quite happy, Livia Ussaro existed and was telling him interesting, extraordinary things, even though it wasn't clear exactly what she was telling him.

'No, I wanted to make the experiment for purposes of social study. I was born with a weakness for sociology. When the other girls couldn't wait to put on long sheer stockings, I was reading Pareto and what's worse, understanding him. Unfortunately, Pareto doesn't have much to say about women, nor do the other sociologists. As a woman, I'm interested in female sociology, and one of the most important problems in that field is prostitution. The first thing to realise is that you can't understand prostitution, really understand it, if you haven't been a prostitute: if you haven't, at least once, performed an act of prostitution.'

He had the feeling he was at a lecture, at some convention of intellectuals, and he ordered two more beers: he had never got drunk on beer, but he feared that tonight he might have to.

'It isn't a logically incontrovertible theory,' she continued, cool, magisterial, and yet so feminine, 'in fact, if you analyse it closely it doesn't hold up at all, but it has its charm. The experiment I wanted to do was to go out on the street, let a man accost me and go with him for money. In that way I would have a typical experience, a sample experience, empirical but significant data that would help me study the question. Except that, whenever I was about to do so, two or three thousand years of taboos stopped me. In addition, I was a virgin and the part of my ego that belonged to the herd balked at the idea of losing my virginity for science. Then, at the age of twenty, despite my frigidity, I fell in love, it was a strange thing that only lasted two days. In those two days the man who had succeeded in breaking down my defences took full advantage of the situation, I lost my virginity, and so there was no longer anything to prevent me performing my experiment. But it took me until I was twenty-three before I managed to overcome all the taboos. And it happened by chance.'

Everything had a slightly hallucinatory air, including all that gold, and that startling silence of an area of Milan a little way out of the centre, towards midnight, when only a few cars pass, the odd tram, and there are long minutes of silence as if you are in the garden of a seventeenth-century villa.

'I was in the Piazza della Scala, that evening, waiting for a tram,' she said, informatively, 'it was about this time of night, I'd been to see a friend who's a dressmaker, a really stupid girl, but a good worker, even though she only ever talks about pleats, or about her molars, which are always hurting her. I was depressed and all at once I realised that a man about forty was coming towards me, swaying as he walked. I stayed where I was, and he told me in German that I was the most beautiful brunette he'd ever seen anywhere in Europe. I told him, in German, that I didn't like drunks and asked him to leave me alone. Then he took off his hat, in that heat he was wearing a beautiful black straw hat, and told me he was happy I knew German, and that he was sorry but he wasn't drunk, maybe I hadn't seen him properly, he simply had a limp. You can understand the remorse I felt, I'd told him he was drunk, when all he had was a limp. In the meantime he asked if he could buy me something. I said yes, by way of apology. He took me to the Biffi, I had an ice cream, and then he told me that he was feeling lonely and asked if I could keep him company. I said yes. Then he said, *"Für Geld oder für Sympathie?"* He was a German, after all, and didn't appreciate equivocation, he wanted to know if I would keep him company for free, as my friend the dressmaker says, out of sympathy, or for money. I was thinking about my prostitution experiment and immediately said, *"Für Geld."* He asked me how much, it was my chance to carry out my sociological experiment, but the financial side of it was something I had no idea about. I told him the lowest figure, I was afraid that otherwise he'd say no.'

'How much?' The most fascinating form of madness was the lucid, rational kind.

'Five thousand.' She paused.

'And then?'

'Nothing. He gave it to me immediately. His car was parked in the Piazza della Scala, he asked me to tell him where to go: it was a bit awkward, because I didn't know anything about the sexual geography of Milan at the time. By chance, we ended up in the Parco Lambro.' She fell silent again.

'And then?'

'What struck me was how quick it was.' She was very serious now. 'And later, every time I repeated these experiments, it was the one thing I could never understand, the brevity. I think it takes longer to weigh yourself properly on a pharmacist's weighing machine. And to think that four-fifths of human experience is based on something so quick, something that flashes by in an instant. I wrote lots of notes about that first experiment, but you wouldn't want to read them.'

No, he didn't want to, but he didn't tell her that. 'Is that what led up to your meeting Alberta?'

'Yes, it is. In fact, I met her the very next day. A friend from university had invited me to a cocktail party. His father is the director of a large company making corsets and swimming costumes, and they were presenting their latest creations to the press and public in a reception room in the Hotel Principe. I'd never been to anything like that before, so I went. There were a whole lot of women, and many must have been lesbians, real lesbians, because they kept coming up to me and buzzing around me like flies until they realised I wasn't the rose they'd imagined and left me alone. Then, in the middle of that world that was so strange to me, I saw someone else looking as lost as I was. That was her, Alberta. I don't have friends, I've never been good at making them, but after an hour Alberta and I were like sisters and we'd told each other everything. It was the first time since high school that I'd found someone I could talk to about general topics, I don't mean the future of mankind, but at least the influence in politics of the female vote. These days, the only general topics people talk about are leisure time and the influence of machines, which apart from anything else aren't even really what you could call topics, in the strict sense of the term. Don't you agree?'

He did, warmly, maybe because he was still warm with beer: leisure time and the influence of machines, pah!

'We left the cocktail party and she took me to her place, at eleven we were still talking, about midnight we realised we hadn't eaten and she prepared some bread and cheese, and at half past one we were still there, talking.'

'And what did you talk about?' Four or five hours of

conversation: it might well be that they'd done nothing but talk, Livia Ussaro said so, and Livia Ussaro didn't tell lies, but a lesbian may use the word for something more intimate. The suspicion, though, faded immediately, because of the fervour with which she answered his question.

'I think that in the last three hours all we talked about was prostitution. I told her about my experiment the previous night—that's why I had to tell you what led up to our meeting—and Alberta told me that over the past few months she'd been doing the same kind of experiment. Not for the purposes of study, obviously, but out of necessity. Not long after she had arrived in Milan from Naples, she had realised it wouldn't be easy to live here. She'd wanted to work in the theatre, but she'd given up the idea after talking to the porters of the theatres where the various companies worked. Instead, she easily found work as a shop assistant, because of her elegant figure and the way she treated the customers, but the customers, or the boss, sooner or later put her in a position where she had to be fired. So, when she was really broke, she'd go out and come back home a little later feeling a little easier financially. I made her tell me all the experiences she'd had, half my notes are based on what Alberta told me. If people here in Italy didn't laugh about certain subjects, especially if dealt with by a woman, I could write a report on private prostitution. There was one question that fascinated us above all: From a social point of view, does a woman have the right to prostitute herself, but, I emphasise, privately? And only when she wants to, without anything else driving her?'

He must be drunk and he was still thirsty. He wanted to see if she would get angry. 'A woman also has the right to get married, at least so I've heard.'

She didn't get angry, but she seemed disappointed. 'Don't turn nasty on me, I'm serious. For an intelligent woman, like Alberta, like many others . . .'

'Like you.'

'Yes, like me, too. It's difficult to get married when you're intelligent. Of course, in the end we all get married, but an intelligent woman wants to marry well, and it's difficult to find the right man.'

He really wanted to make her angry. 'That's not a good reason to go out on the streets and let yourself be picked up by the first man who comes along.'

'You're doing this deliberately. I'm not saying she has to do that, I'm just asking, theoretically, whether or not she has the right.'

He had let her talk for a long time and had learned something useful: Alberta Radelli had indulged in private prostitution, a form of prostitution that seemed to be on the increase. But he needed to know more. 'Listen, I like general topics very much, but for the job I'm doing I need details. Do you have any idea where Alberta went to pose for these photographs, and why?'

When she thought, her face took on an almost child-ish expression. 'I don't have a very good memory, but I do remember something about it because it was the reason I became disappointed in Alberta.'

'What is it you remember?' If he could find out who

had taken those photographs, there was no stopping him.

'I remember a number. Numbers are easier to remember, you know. For example, I remember they were giving her thirty thousand lire to pose for those photographs. I spent a whole afternoon arguing with her, she really disappointed me, although she realised those photographs were something different . . .'

Oh, no, enough philosophy for the moment. He interrupted her. 'What's the number you remember?'

'The number is 78, it was a house number, but I don't remember the name of the street. I asked her for the details, because I realised there was something that wasn't right, that she was moving from private prostitution into something organised . . .'

No, no, he interrupted her again, he would take her to the Torre Branca one of these days, on a rainy weekday, and there he would let her talk about general topics, there in the deserted round bar a hundred metres above the Milanese plain, until the place closed, but now he needed to know about Alberta, and quickly.

'Now please listen, this is very important. Can you remember anything more about these photographs? The number 78 isn't enough, and we have to find the photographer, soon.' Why soon? A year had passed since Alberta's death, what was the hurry? Maybe he was telepathic or something, but he felt a sense of urgency.

'I don't remember anything else, she just told me she was going to see a photographer.'

'Obviously.'

'Oh, wait, she said something strange, now I remember, she said it was like industrial photography. What has industrial photography got to do with nude photographs?'

It did have something to do with it, but he didn't tell her: it was a cover. So, at number 78 of one of the three thousand or six thousand streets in Milan there existed, or at least there had existed a year before, a studio for industrial photography, at which, discreetly, artistic photographs were also taken. It might take Mascaranti only half a day to find this studio, if it still existed, or even if it didn't.

'And did she tell you who had suggested she pose for these photographs?'

'Yes, she did. It was a filthy business, I don't like perversions.' She looked at the barman, who was standing restlessly in the doorway of the bar, waiting to close: it was almost midnight. 'There was a man who'd approached her, they'd gone in his car some distance from Milan, he was a middle-aged man, I think, he was very generous and very kind, but he'd hardly touched her. Then he'd confessed to her that at his age people had weaknesses, he was able to respond to female charms more in a beautiful photograph, if she wanted to pose for some photographs that would be sufficient for him, just photographs. She said yes, and he gave her the address of the photographer. Then he asked her if she had a friend who might also like to pose for photographs, each of them would be given thirty thousand lire.'

It was a lot of money just so that this voyeur could look at some photographs. 'Let's see if I've got this right. Alberta told you that a man she'd been with suggested she pose for some photographs and gave her the address of a photographer. In other words, Alberta had to go alone to this photographer, who already knew the work he had to do?'

'Yes, that's exactly it.'

'But, in order to let the photographer know that she had come for that special kind of photograph, didn't she have to tell him anything, give him some kind of password? She couldn't just tell him, out of the blue, that she wanted to be photographed nude.'

'No, she didn't need to say anything, that was why I quarrelled with Alberta. I made her give me all the details because I wanted to understand what it was all about. All Alberta had to do was go to the studio and when she got there she didn't have to tell him anything, the photographer already knew. She would pose for some photographs, the photographer would pay her, and that was it.'

For a moment he could hear sirens sounding the alarm, just like when he was a little boy during the war. 'Try to remember: was the photographer supposed to hand over the exposed film to Alberta, or was he supposed to keep it for himself and send Alberta away? And are you sure, or do you have any doubts?'

'I think I'm sure.' Oh, that thoughtful little girl's face of hers. 'Alberta told me all she had to do was go to the studio, pose for the photographs, and that was it, she thought it was stupid to pass up all that money for a matter of principle and she was even going to take a friend of hers, Maurilia, and I told her that if she went and posed for those photographs I never wanted to see her again.'

It was time to go, the barman and a large man who had suddenly appeared told them they were going to close. So he took his Livia Ussaro outside, pushed her into the Giulietta, but didn't switch the engine on. Once the shutters of the bar had been pulled down, that stretch of the Via Plinio was quite shadowy and discreet.

'I'm not going to let you go home to sleep if you don't explain one point,' he said, perhaps a little too seriously. 'In Alberta's handbag on the evening before the day she was found dead in Metanopoli, there was a Minox cartridge that hadn't yet been developed. Do you know what that means?'

'I'm thinking about it.'

'Let me do the thinking. It means the photographer gave the cartridge to Alberta.'

'Obviously.'

'Right. But what was Alberta supposed to do with it? Did she have to take it to that photosensitive middle-aged man?' How witty he was!

Livia smiled, it was nice, talking like this in the semi-darkness of the car, the Via Plinio was more deserted than ever. 'No, that's not possible, I'm sure of it. Apart from anything else she couldn't have known where the man who'd spoken to her about the photos lived; when a woman goes with a man like that he doesn't normally give her his address. This one certainly didn't.'

'They may have fixed a place to meet so that she could hand the cartridge over to him to be developed.' The hypothesis was almost ridiculous: when a photographer takes photographs, it's normal for him to develop, enlarge and print them himself, without the person who wanted those photographs having to look for another photographer or make the enlargements himself, which would have been quite difficult for an amateur, given that the photographs had been taken on Minox film.

'No, Alberta would have told me if she'd had to hand over the roll of film to that man. I questioned her for two hours, I was very afraid, I realised it was no longer private prostitution, that she was going downhill, that she was getting mixed up in . . .'

He wasn't listening to her, even though he would have liked to, because he would have liked to talk to her for weeks, about all her beloved 'general topics,' but he was imagining Alberta and her blonde friend going to the photographer, getting undressed, posing for the photographs, then taking the money and leaving. That was the logical sequence. Instead of which, Alberta had the cartridge in her handbag. What was she supposed to do with it? And why had the photographer given it to her?

'You're not listening to me, are you?'

'No.'

Humbly, generously, she said, 'Ask me more about Alberta.'

Yes, he did have other questions to ask. 'After that time when she told you she was going to pose for photographs, what did Alberta say to you when you saw her again?'

'I never saw her again. Nearly a week later, I read in the newspaper that she'd killed herself.'

The path ended here. 'We need to meet again, do you mind that?'

'No, even if it's only about Alberta.' Then she betrayed her feminine weakness. 'Why are you so interested in her? You never met her, you're not even a policeman, in fact, you told me you're taking a big risk, getting involved in these things.'

At last he looked at her without thinking about Alberta. 'I can tell you, Little Miss General Topics, it's because of a general topic.'

'And what would that be?'

He could tell her, in fact she was the one person in the world he could tell something like that without making her smile. 'I don't like swindlers.' He then explained what he meant, he even had to generalise a bit to thank her for all the useful information she had given him. 'Society is a game, right? The rules of the game are written in the penal code, in the civil code, and in another rather imprecise, unwritten code called the moral code. They may be debatable codes, and have to be constantly updated, but either you keep to the rules, or you don't. The only person breaking the rules of the game that I can respect is the bandit with his rifle hiding in the mountains: he doesn't keep to the rules of the game, but then he makes it quite clear he doesn't want to play in good society anyway and that he'll make his own rules as he wants, with his rifle. But not swindlers, no, I hate and despise them. These days, there are bandits with lawyers in attendance, they cheat, they rob, they kill, but they've already worked out a line of defence with their lawyer in case they're found out and put on trial, and they never get the punishment they deserve. They want others to keep to the game, to the rules, but not themselves. I don't like that, I can't stand these people, just knowing they're near, just smelling them, sets my nerves on edge.'

She would have liked to continue this conversation, she loved hearing that kind of speech, but tenderly he asked her where he could take her and she replied, just to her front door, over there opposite the bar, and then told him that he could phone her whenever he wanted, she'd be very pleased to hear from him, and her voice was definitely not the voice of a frigid woman, but he had to go, he had left Davide alone too long.

Davide was lying on the bed, fully dressed apart from his shoes, the light was on and he was awake. On the table were the bottle of Frascati, which looked empty, and the bottle of whisky, which was open but from which only a couple of spoonfuls at most seemed to be missing, in what must have been an extreme effort of will Davide had drunk less than a spoonful of whisky an hour, even though he'd had the bottle there at his disposal, as well as his doctor's permission.

He took the chair and moved it close to the bed. Davide made as if to sit up, it wasn't right to lie down when his doctor was here, but Duca put a hand on his shoulder and made him lie down again. 'Davide,' he said, 'we need to sleep.' He had been happy with Livia Ussaro, and he was happy now with Davide Auseri, the psychotic only-begotten son of a leading engineer. It had been a happy evening. 'We can't spend our days and nights thinking about a woman, especially if she's dead. You're still thinking about Alberta, aren't you?'

Davide turned his face to the pillow: in his language, that meant yes.

'It isn't right, Davide.' He was doing his job as a doctor, with passion, with happiness. 'It isn't right for someone of your age to be in love with a dead woman. I'm going to talk to you a little about her, because these past few days I've understood a lot of things. When you threw Alberta out of your car, you weren't in love with her. When you read in the newspapers that she'd killed herself, you still weren't in love with her, but you felt remorse. Later, the remorse grew in you, more every day, every time you got drunk, but it didn't stay as just remorse. Over time, alongside the remorse another feeling was born. Let's call it love. You kept thinking, "If I'd taken her with me that day, I'd have saved her life." Then you went further, you started to think that if you'd taken her with you, not only would you have saved her life, but it would have been beautiful for both of you, really beautiful, not just making love so much, but something more. You've never had a girlfriend, you've never really been in love, the upbringing your father gave you, your father's personality, have always crushed you. Alberta was the first woman who gave you this feeling of love, this need for love—after she was dead, unfortunately. I know this is all rather like street-corner psychoanalysis, but that's the way it is: you keep thinking about Alberta because you're in love with her, and being in love with her what you can't stand is the thought that she's dead and you were partly responsible, am I right or not?'

He had hoped it would happen, without really expecting it: but now he was pleased to see that Davide was beginning to cry. Even though he covered his eyes and no sound came from him, he couldn't conceal the fact, because his large chest was heaving. Calmly, Duca went on, 'Since the dead never come back, and neither I nor anyone else can bring Alberta here to you, alive, and have her cure you, as only she could do, then we have to do something else. The most important thing is to find the person who forced her to kill herself, or who killed her, and when we find him we strangle him. Just tell yourself that: we'll find him and strangle him. I might leave the job to you.' He had to appeal to his baser instincts, in order to save him. 'It isn't hard, you'll see, and you won't spend even one day in prison. We'll find this person and you'll strangle him, just like that, with your bare hands, you won't even have to squeeze hard, I'll explain to you some other time, as a doctor, when you can be sure you've strangled him, the kind of cracking you have to feel between your fingers as you squeeze, and after that cracking you can even relax your grip because there's nothing more to be done. Of course you'll say you were attacked, the person jumped you, he had a knife, a revolver, you were forced to defend yourself, you were about to be killed and you had to react. There'll be irrefutable witnesses, Mascaranti for example, I assure you that you'll be able to strangle that man without any problem. And I assure you it'll happen soon, because we'll find him soon, but now you have to sleep, you have to relax, to be ready for that moment.' It wasn't a nice little bedtime story, but the child he had to put to sleep was rather big and needed stronger stories. He, Duca, also needed a bedtime story, one about finding a photographer in the woods. He just had to find out who had taken those photographs, only that, nothing but that.

3

The taxi stopped at 78 Via Farini and Alberta and Maurilia got out. The front door of number 78 was large and a lorry was coming out, behind the taxi, then there was a tram ringing its bell, and only after an exchange of imprecations between the lorry driver, the tram driver and the taxi driver, did they reach the caretaker's wife, who told them that *Industry Photographic* was on the second floor, the staircase beyond the courtyard, and they crossed that courtyard, watched hungrily by a number of men in overalls who were loading a lorry with metal disks and pursued by sibilant phrases from these men, indicating what they would like to do with the two girls if they could, propositions which in themselves weren't unnatural or wicked, just ill-timed.

On the second floor, the young man who opened the door was simply a young man in a white dressing gown, in other words, he had a face without any distinguishing characteristics, almost like one of those faces drawn by someone who doesn't know how to draw at all, and the only things you could say about him were that he wasn't old and that he wasn't wearing a black dressing gown.

He looked at them and didn't say anything, they didn't say anything, and he let them in. There were no windows in the first room, and the light was on.

'This way,' he said.

The second room was a long, large room, there were two

windows, but the blinds were closed, you could see strips of sunlight through the dusty panes, which were also closed, and the light was on in here, too.

'You can undress over there,' he said, indicating a corner with a table and chairs. 'Don't knock the chess pieces over.' On the table there was a chessboard, with a dozen pieces, the others were in a wooden box.

'Isn't there a screen?' Alberta asked, and immediately realised she was an idiot, of course there wasn't. There was nothing that looked anything like a screen in that long gallery that was supposed to be a photographic studio, or any furniture for that matter, apart from that table and chairs which were infinitely, obviously temporary. It was all quite frightening: those closed windows, the lights on at eleven in the morning, that heat as dead as a tomb in the sun.

'I'm sorry,' the young man said, referring, apparently, to the fact that he didn't have a screen. 'But don't worry, the doors are locked.' He had reached the far end of the gallery, and his voice, a voice as nondescript as his face, echoed a little.

'Can't we open the windows?' Alberta yelled towards the dark end of the room. Within a minute, both the girls were soaked in sweat, their clothes clinging to them.

'Then more heat will come in, along with the stench of acetylene,' the man with the nondescript face said, and all at once the end of the gallery burst into flame: he had lit the three standing lamps and the six lights on the ceiling. 'I don't know what they make down there, but they use acetylene, and the smell is ghastly.'

'Who wants to pose first?' he asked. 'It's all the same to me.'

Maurilia was a blonde who laughed easily, got scared easily, was easy with everything. Now she was scared. 'You start,' she said to Alberta.

Alberta undressed quickly, her dress, bra, and knickers ending up on a chair, she kept on her high-heeled shoes, not to make the photographs sexier, but in order not to have to walk barefoot on that floor.

'Over here,' the man said. In front of the floodlights was a background of clouds, an enlarged photograph mounted on a sliding door. 'We'll be quick, with this little camera, you'll see.'

Only then did Alberta see the heavy tripod, and on the tripod something resembling a cigarette lighter, which must be the camera.

'Stand over there, on that rug.' He stooped behind the cigarette lighter and started looking. 'You choose the poses, it doesn't matter very much, hide your face if you want, but you have to show it in at least five or six of the shots. Move about as you want, it's like being in a film, come on.' In his left hand he held the shaft of the tripod, making the Minox move imperceptibly in every direction he wanted, and in his right hand he held a wire with a button that worked the shutter. 'Move, one,' click, 'there, stop, two,' click, with each photograph that cigarette lighter closed and reopened, just as if lighting a cigarette, 'move, stop, three,' click, and so it went on, four, five, ten, twelve photographs, every now and again he suggested a more aggressive pose, but always in words that were restrained, clean, without vulgarity, 'move, stop, twenty-six, that's enough, now it's your friend's turn.'

At the other end of the gallery, in the nauseating heat, Maurilia was afraid. Not of undressing. She wasn't even sure what she was afraid of. Alberta knew her: on the surface she was a carefree blonde, she had immediately agreed to pose in the nude, but now she was looking at Alberta imploringly.

'If you don't want to do it, then don't,' she said irritably, she couldn't stand stupidity and Maurilia was a champion of stupidity: flabby, morally shifty, sure to end up badly, although she, Alberta, tried to keep her from the slippery slope that led to walking the avenues every night, with a parasite a few metres away keeping watch over you only to take the money you just earned. But for now she was bound to her, as if they were married.

'Look, you're here now, just pose,' said the young man in the dressing gown, who had heard these last words.

His tone wasn't threatening, at least on the surface, only sad, as if he was saying, 'What a pity, she came here to pose for photographs, and now she doesn't want to,' yet Alberta heard something else in it. What the man who wasn't old and wasn't wearing a black dressing gown was actually saying, Alberta was sure, was, 'Now that you're here you're going to pose, even if you don't want to, because I want you to.'

With a forlorn smile, Maurilia said, 'No, no, no,' she undressed and Alberta walked with her to the end of the room, where the man was waiting, in the shadow, against the flaming background of the floodlights.

'On the rug, there, like that,' he said, becoming quite

pleasant again, 'do whatever you like, just don't come off the rug, but on it you can move, like that, stop, one,' and the clicks started again, 'move, there, stop, two, move, not the same pose, something different, there, stop, three.'

Alberta started to smell the hot, metallic smell of the floodlights, Maurilia's nudity was irritating, at least for a woman: aesthetically, her body was overblown, poorly arranged, it seemed to have been constructed for one purpose only, a sexual one, her arms and legs and head and shoulders and hair seemed as much like sexual organs as the actual sexual organs. She stopped looking and thinking that she, too, had posed like that: seeing it from the outside, it was more indecent than she had thought. She turned back towards the other end of the room, partly so as not to be blinded by the floodlights, and only then did she notice that along one of the two longer walls there ran a narrow shelf on which stood, in a row, objects she couldn't make out immediately, and when she did make them out her first thought was that they were toys: lorries, tipper trucks, tractors, other vehicles, maybe agricultural ones, each one about ten centimetres long at most. She picked up a silver tanker lorry, she was puzzled at first, but then it struck her that the imitation was perfect, these weren't toys, they were industrial models.

'They're nice, aren't they, but don't touch,' the young man said, he obviously had eyes in the back of his head, all the while continuing to take photographs, 'yes, yes, move, there, good, stop, twelve.'

Go on, she thought, what did she care about the models,

she was drowning in the heat and the bad smell, and in her anger towards herself, but it was much more than anger, much more than contempt, much more than disgust, almost hate, and perhaps more.

Finally the photographer said, 'Move, stop, twenty-five,' and for the last time there was a click, and Maurilia came and got dressed again next to Alberta, who was looking at the chessboard: it was an endgame study, white to move and win. Next to the chessboard there was a little English chess magazine: the young man was clearly a fan of the great game.

'You play chess?' The man had switched off the flood-lights at the far end and had come towards them, fiddling with his little photographic cigarette lighter.

'I was the best in my school.'

He finally managed to take that little object out of the cigarette lighter—it was almost like a little telephone receiver for a doll, two small spools joined on one side by a strip of metal—and put it down next to the chessboard together with the camera. Something spiritual went through him, or rather through his hands, they started dancing over the chessboard with an airy lightness. 'So maybe you've under-stood where the trick is. There are two white pawns on the seventh rank ready to move forward, but the attacking move can't be from these pawns, I think the white king has to move to a square where he can escape being constantly checked by the black rook.'

She had already worked out the same move, but it revolted her to tell that to this disgusting individual. She hadn't seen a chessboard for about ten years: it took her back to her days at boarding school, the nuns' habits rustling as they walked through the dormitories, the cold winter mornings in the frozen church, the mass that seemed endless, torn as she was between her lingering sleepiness and her growing hunger, and the recreation period in the hall on rainy days, with competitions for reading, sewing, draughts, chess, because they must have been sporting nuns with a strong competitive spirit. And because of that memory, the only decent thing in this indecent place was that abstract, geometric object with those symbolic wooden pieces. 'No, I think the first move should actually be the advancement of a white pawn,' she said, but not to him, it was as if she was talking to one of her classmates at school, a long way from this place and this time and this Maurilia who was laboriously, clumsily clothing her sexuality again, stumbling over the hooks of her bra which she seemed unable to do up.

'But then the black rook will capture the advanced pawn and the white king will be in check,' he said. For a moment there was a very different thought in the way he looked at her: 'I didn't know whores were so good at chess.'

'I don't think so,' she said. She could still hear the rain pouring in the beautiful, or maybe not so beautiful but at least quiet, recreation hall on those long-gone days, and she was sad that she couldn't remember the classmates she'd played chess with, their faces, their voices, anything. 'Because the white bishop—'

'The white bishop can't avoid capture by the rook,' he interrupted her, passionately, and there was something disgusting even in that intellectual passion.

'I didn't mean that the bishop could avoid capture by the rook,' she replied curtly. 'I meant that the bishop goes here, to f8 and allows the pawn on g7 to go forward, free from the rook's attack.' Unfortunately, Maurilia, having finally arranged her bra, had approached her, and was almost leaning on her now, her warm damp body still anxious for proximity, protection, assurance that she had not been forgotten, and the soft noise of the rain coming from the garden of the school faded immediately in Alberta. She looked at that hungry, demanding human being in a significant way.

'Oh, yes, the money,' he said without smiling, 'I'll be right back, then I'll see if your theory about the bishop works, I think it might.'

He went into the next room, and Alberta, with an instinctive gesture, took that little object composed of two round wheels. She had understood clearly what it was and what it contained: the film with the repugnant photographs of two unfortunate naked women, and one of the two unfortunate women was her, perhaps more than Maurilia, who at least didn't really know, and would never really know, what was happening to her.

'There, thirty for you,' the young man said, coming back from the other room, his eyes still a little distant, in the world of that chess problem, and in his hand were two envelopes, the promised reward had been put gallantly into envelopes, and he gave one envelope to her and the other to Maurilia, 'and thirty for you.' At the door, before they went out, he said to her, 'If the bishop's move is right, then you're really good, I'd been thinking about it all morning and hadn't found it.' He closed the door behind them impatiently, came back into the room, lit a cigarette and stared at the chessboard. So, first move e7 pawn to e8, which promotes to a queen. But the black rook immediately captures the queen. At this point the bishop enters the scene, in other words a3 to f8, he moved the bishop to f8 and immediately saw that it worked like that: the rook had the white king in check . . . No, he couldn't, because after the third check he had to give himself up to the bishop, and no other move black made, with any piece, could stop the second white pawn from advancing, and white winning the game. Exactly as the girl had said. Pleased, but a little irritated that a girl like that should know more about chess than he did, he picked up the Minox from its place next to the chessboard and looked for the cartridge, but it wasn't there, not even among the other chess pieces. He didn't look hard, he was quite intelligent, and he'd already figured it out. He couldn't run after the girls, it had been about ten minutes, he'd been ensnared by the chessboard, that filthy brunette had done it by luring him with the chess pieces.

Despite the heat, he never sweated, but at that moment he started to sweat. Slowly he put the chess pieces back in their box, thinking, if his anxiety could be called thinking, put the magazine on the chessboard and the box with the pieces on the magazine, tidily, but his disgusting hands were shaking, then he made up his mind and went to the phone hanging on the wall next to the door.

Which was why, when Alberta got out of the taxi in front

of her building, after having seen Maurilia home, she saw a young man waiting, who was very well-dressed in a light Prince of Wales check suit, and a faded yellow tie, his hair was thick but very tidy and he had a kind smile. He looked a little short-sighted.

'Excuse me, signorina.'

Here in the Viale Montenero, at a quarter past one in the afternoon, everyone was at lunch, at least those few people who had stayed in Milan. There was literally nobody in the street, almost as if they had never existed or couldn't exist in that heat. Every now and again a car passed, and in about ten minutes a tram might pass along the ring road. She stopped, calmly aggressive, because it had never occurred to her to take liberties in the area where she lived, and she stopped partly because the young man was barring her way, not only with his body, but also with his myopic but feral look, which was in marked contrast to his polite smile.

'I'm sorry, signorina, but I think you have a roll of film in your handbag, a roll of film you took half an hour ago from a photographer's studio. Do you mind giving it back to me?' and he even held out his hand in ironic trustfulness. His face, which seemed fat even though it wasn't, it was the powerful slab-like jaws that gave that impression of fat, turned nasty only for a moment, just to show her that she should be afraid.

As in fact she was afraid, but didn't show it, nobody could force her to yield, even a single abrupt word provoked a cold, irrepressible rebelliousness in her.

'I don't know you, I haven't taken anything, I don't know what you're talking about, leave me alone or I'll start screaming.'

'Go ahead and scream,' he said, very calmly, taking her hand and trying to push her. 'While you're screaming let's get in this car, it'll be easier to talk there.'

A car passed, she did not scream, but resisted the push. 'I really am going to scream.'

'Maybe you are. And maybe we'll both end up in a police station. I wouldn't like that to happen, and I don't think you would either. On the other hand, if you give me that roll of film, I'll leave immediately and you'll avoid lots of things. Apart from the police, you'll avoid vitriol being thrown in your face.' He tried again to push her towards the Mercedes 230 parked a dozen metres further along the street, but Alberta suddenly escaped from him with a jerk that was unexpectedly strong in a woman and ran into the dark, hot entrance hall of her building, ran up the stairs, first floor, second, third, looked over the banisters, no, the man wasn't following her, she would have time to open the door to her apartment, her sister was at the phone company, she didn't come home for lunch. She managed to open it, went in, closed the door, and all at once felt ashamed: she felt contempt for her own fear when the man had grabbed her arm.

She went into the living room and looked out of the window at the street, through the blinds incrusted with year-old dust. There was nobody there and nobody was passing, even the Mercedes 230 had gone.

She wouldn't give in, never. Livia was right, she didn't

want to descend into that cesspit, she would go to the police, hand over the film, and tell them everything, the middle-aged man in the Flaminia, he had even said he would get her a job as a shop assistant in Hamburg, but what kind of shop assistant? It was so easy to understand, but the nausea was too much: enough now.

She looked in the kitchen for something to eat, then stretched out on one of the two little beds with the bears and dogs and butterflies on the headboard, and even managed to fall asleep, then woke up, in the silence, in the stifling heat of mid-afternoon, and after she had been awake a few seconds, just like that, in the silence, the telephone rang.

Maybe it was Livia, she needed Livia, she had to tell her everything. She got up and went to the phone.

'Alberta, Alberta.'

'Yes, it's me.' It was Maurilia. The most scared voice she had ever heard, the voice of terror.

'It's Maurilia, Alberta, it's Maurilia.'

'I hear you, what is it? Where are you?' She was not afraid yet, or rather, she didn't want to be afraid.

'It's Maurilia, Alberta, it's Maurilia.'

'What's happening? What's wrong?'

A man's voice replied, and she recognised it even though she had heard it only once and it had only said a few words.

'I think you recognised your friend Maurilia's voice.' His tone was even more threatening than before.

She didn't reply, but he went on, knowing that she had heard him perfectly well. 'You just have to take that roll of film back to the studio where you were this morning.

Right now, because the photographer is waiting for it. You wouldn't want anything unpleasant to happen to your friend Maurilia. Don't pretend you don't understand, that'll only make it worse for you and your friend.'

She did not reply, she was about to shout out that she would go there, immediately, but with the police, only she couldn't, because they had hung up at the other end. That was when she understood what was happening.

4

Everything was going wrong, the only thing that worked was the air conditioning in those two rooms in the Hotel Cavour, cool without being damp and without smelling odd; everything was going badly wrong in a way that the confident, efficient Milanese who passed, sweating, along the Via Fatebenefratelli or through the Piazza Cavour couldn't begin to imagine, even though they read stories like this every day in the *Corriere*. For them, these stories belonged to a fourth dimension, devised by an Einstein of crime, who was even more incomprehensible than the Einstein of physics. What was real, for those people in the street, was going to the tobacconist to buy filter cigarettes, so that they didn't feel so bad about smoking, and every now and again thinking about the next morning, the office, the work that had to be finished before the boss summoned them, or looking for a moment at those two girls standing alone waiting for the tram, with their low-cut tops. These were the natural dimensions of life, the rest they only read about and were as evanescent as things you only read about, *he stabbed his wife 27 times*, or else, *housewife with five children involved in vast drug ring*, or else *gunfight between rival gangs in Viale Monza*, all this was only reading, quite stimulating, but then they went back home and found the gas bill waiting to be paid. No, down there on the street, they couldn't imagine how bad things were, even though up here they seemed like four carving forks with all those plates on the table filled with canapés, rolls, breadsticks with the tips covered in sweet ham from San Daniele, vases of butter in ice, rounds of pâté and bottles of beer in small silver buckets.

The only one wearing a jacket was Davide, and maybe he was the only other thing that was working apart from the air conditioning: suddenly in his life he had encountered beer, it had been an abrupt, passionate encounter, which greatly accelerated the detoxifying therapy, beer might be fattening, but someone like Davide would need a whole barrel of it before he got fat. As his alcohol intake decreased, Davide was slowly regaining the power of speech and a kind of masculine energy. Just then, he said, with a glass coaster in his hand, 'Doesn't anybody want the pâté?' and offered it around.

Mascaranti shook his head, and so did Carrua, because he was there, too, also without a jacket, chewing rather than smoking his cigarette. And Duca also shook his head, and looked tenderly at Davide as he spread pâté on a small slice of bread. Ten more days, more or less, and his patient would be able to live happily on mineral water and milk.

'Let's start from the beginning,' Carrua said, putting the cigarette down in the saucer of his filter coffee. 'With the photographer.'

Mascaranti still had his little notebook in his hand. 'He's gone,' he said. 'There was nothing left at 78 Via Farini the day before Alberta Radelli's death, it was all above board. The two rooms had been rented by a German more than a year earlier, but the landlord and caretaker of the building had seen this German only a couple of times, the only person working in the studio was a young man, a friend of the German, who told the caretaker his name was Caserli, or Caselli, but he's not sure, because he didn't see him often. Both the young man and the other man vanished into thin air a year ago.'

'We should be able to track down the German,' Carrua said, 'you can't rent premises without giving your particulars.'

'Of course he gave them, here they are,' and Mascaranti read, with a vague southern accent, a series of syllables coming from thousands of years back in the Black Forest, which his accent made a little genteel. 'It's an invented name and address, at least the police in Bonn, where this guy was supposed to be living, say there's no name like it either in the official register of the city or in their own records.'

All that effort on the part of Mascaranti to find the studio, knowing nothing but the number, 78, and then when he had found it, there hadn't been anybody or anything there for a year, nor had any trace been left behind.

'One thing is clear,' Duca said, mainly to Carrua, but also to Mascaranti, 'to have rented those rooms using a false name, and then to have unfurnished it so quickly in the days after Alberta Radelli's death, they must have considered the work they were doing there very important, and if the work consisted of taking photographs of naked women the caretaker must have seen girls going in and out.'

'Yes, I questioned the caretaker's wife, too,' Mascaranti said. 'Girls did pass through every now and again, but not very often, and she even told me what they were doing, she and her husband had gone a couple of times to see, the young man had invited them up. They were photographing little model cars, trucks, harvesters, she told me, and sometimes the girls were there as background, they use women to advertise all kinds of things these days.'

A cover: industrial photos meaning nude photos. It had stood up very well, for more than a year, under the eyes of the police, and it had stood up even after they disappeared, so that Mascaranti had spent all evening seething with anger.

'Now let's talk about the other girl,' Carrua said.

The police often succeed through repetition, by repeating that two plus two equals four in the end you discover something more, but there wasn't anything more to be discovered about Maurilia.

'Maurilia Arbati,' Mascaranti read in the notebook, 'twenty-seven years old, worked at La Rinascente, in the department selling fabrics, towels, that kind of thing.'

Twenty-seven: in the Minox photos she didn't look it, she had reached the age of twenty-seven as a nice, hard-working girl, the personnel department at the store had never had to reprimand her, and suddenly at that relatively advanced age, she enters the dark world of adventure.

So Mascaranti goes to La Rinascente and gets to talk to the right manager.

'Impossible, do you know how many girls there are here?' the manager says. 'How are we going to find her knowing only that her first name is Maurilia?'

'With that,' Mascaranti says, pointing to the telephone that connects to the store's loudspeakers. 'You put out this message, for example: *Signorina Maurilia is asked to report to the manager's office immediately.* Or even better: *Signorina Maurilia, or any of her workmates who knows her, is asked to report to the manager's office immediately.'*

The manager calls a female clerk, she comes in, writes down the message and puts it out, once, twice, three times in succession, then waits three minutes and puts it out again, to all floors, to every corner of the store, through dozens of loudspeakers, so that it's heard by all the people buying feeding bottles, Marie Therese chandeliers, flippers, ties for daddy, they hear the call, soft, not loud, but clear, the name Maurilia perfectly pronounced. As the clerk is just about to put the message out for the third time, the secretary admits a very short fair-haired girl, she doesn't look much more than a child, although there are a number of things to indicate that she isn't.

'Maurilia?' Mascaranti asks.

'No, I'm a friend of hers.'

'This gentleman is from the police,' the manager says sternly. 'Try to answer his questions as accurately as you can.'

'What's Maurilia's surname?' Mascaranti asks.

'Arbati,' the fair-haired girl says.

Triumphantly, Mascaranti writes the name in the little notebook, in three minutes he's tracked down the blonde from the photograph, he's home and dry. 'Where does she live?'

The fair-haired girl hesitates, she's about to say something, and he insists, he's getting impatient: we'll go to where this Maurilia Arbati lives, pick her up, and I'll take her to

Headquarters and there we'll be able to sort this thing out, she posed for the photographs, she'll know who, how, why. 'Where does she live?' he asks curtly.

The girl gets scared and says, '12 Via Nino Bixio,' as accurately as the manager asked.

'You're good friends, right?' Mascaranti asks: to know the address, like that, by heart, they must be good friends. The little fair-haired girl doesn't reply, but it doesn't matter, he has another question to ask: 'Why didn't Maurilia come up here herself? She's the one we called for.'

'Maybe she's off sick,' the manager says.

'She's dead,' the little fair-haired girl says, turning pale, and they make her sit down.

'Why didn't you tell us that before?' Mascaranti wilts: if she's dead he can't question her, and if he can't question her he won't be able to sort anything out at all.

'She died a year ago,' the little fair-haired girl says, 'poor thing, when I heard her name over the loudspeaker just now I felt really bad, after all this time, hearing that they wanted her in the manager's office as if she was still alive.'

She had died very simply, she had left her work without saying anything, even to her, and had gone to Rome, probably with someone—a boyfriend, the little fair-haired girl said, modestly—she had wanted to take a swim, maybe she had been taken ill, and the next day they had found her by the Tiber, just outside Rome, washed up on the river bank like an abandoned boat, in her swimming costume, her clothes in the bushes almost a kilometre further down. The little fair-haired girl had found out from Maurilia's parents when she had phoned them nearly a week later for news of her friend.

So that was the story and Mascaranti had immediately understood. 'What's your name?' he had asked the little fair-haired girl, he had taken all her particulars, then had gone back to Headquarters and phoned Rome. Maurilia Arbati, death by drowning, found in the Tiber at such and such a spot, at such and such a time, by Signor such and such. From the archive he had even had somebody fetch him the Rome newspapers from that date, and read all the items about her he could find, most of which asked the question: Accident or crime? Did she drown or was she killed? You didn't need to be a clairvoyant: in four days the two girls who had posed for the photographs on that Minox film had died, the blonde on the first day, the brunette on the fourth. One on the outskirts of Milan, in Metanopoli, the other near Rome, drowned in the Tiber. Both deaths were curiously ambiguous, one a not entirely convincing suicide, the other an accident that aroused everyone's suspicions.

Now the ambiguity was over, they had died because they had been killed. With a bit of skill the perpetrators had staged Alberta's suicide, she even had a letter in her handbag for her sister in which she asked forgiveness for killing herself—had they forced her to write it, or had she written it earlier, really intending to kill herself? And then a kind of accident for the other girl, Maurilia, an unlikely accident: a young Milanese woman who suddenly goes off to Rome to swim in the Tiber and drowns.

The silent Davide who was getting his voice back even

asked a question: 'But why did they kill one in Milan and one in Rome?' He was a little naïve.

Duca, his doctor, explained it to him, patiently: he was the one person he was patient with. 'Because if in the space of four days, a blonde girl was found drowned here in Milan, in the Lambro, let's say, and then a brunette with her wrists slashed in Metanopoli, the police might link these two rather mysterious deaths and suspect from the start that there was a connection with something bigger. Whereas this way, the dead girl found drowned in Rome couldn't possibly have anything to do, at least for the moment, with the dead girl in Metanopoli. The Rome police investigate their drowned girl and the Milan police their suicide, but they don't find anything because they don't know there's any connection. You were the one who uncovered the connection by handing over that film, you were the one who was with Alberta the day before they killed her.'

'So,' said Davide—some people go from silence to being unable to stop talking—'if I'd handed over that film to the police immediately and told them everything that Alberta had told me, the culprits might have been found immediately.'

'Maybe,' Duca, his clandestine doctor, said. His patient had every possible guilt complex, not a single one escaped him. 'Except that you'd have had to know that the thing Alberta left in your car along with her handkerchief was a cartridge and contained exposed film. But you didn't know that. And your father would have broken your bones one by one as soon as he found out you'd got involved in something like this.' A little laugh from Carrua who knew his powerful friend, Engineer Pietro Auseri, and a knowing smile from Mascaranti. 'You're not guilty of anything. So calm down and pour us some beer.'

'I think we can draw a few conclusions,' Carrua said. 'First point: white slave trade. I don't think there's any doubt.'

No, there wasn't any doubt. Even though he was a doctor and an apostle, he was hungry and finished the few remaining canapés.

'Second point: white slave trade on a large scale. We aren't dealing with a couple of shabby local pimps who've made contact with a couple of shabby pimps from some other country, to exchange a few unfortunate girls. We're dealing with an organised gang of people who'll stop at nothing, who are prepared to kill to prevent their activities getting out. I think that, too, is clear.'

Fairly clear, even though Duca, as an apostle, did not believe in big organisations. There may well be a few rogues here, but good ones, and he already knew where Carrua was going with this. 'All right,' he said, 'you want to inform Interpol, that's perfectly fine. In the end you'll discover everything, but it's going to take a long time because you don't have a lead. These two girls weren't professionals, they were amateurs, two girls working for themselves, two unfortunate girls, but of good family. Every now and again they went out on the streets, but they had no links to the world of prostitution, they didn't have pimps. Their parents, their relatives, their friends don't know anything about their activity, these were girls with jobs and even in the places where they worked everybody talks well of them: serious girls, decent, punctual, in fact they'd have had to have been that way or they'd have been found out after a few weeks. The only lead we have is that film, but we don't know who the photographer was, he's vanished into thin air, and the girls who posed for those photographs are dead. Yes, of course, you'll get these people in the end, but it's going to take a long time. I can't wait that long.'

Another little laugh from Carrua. 'Really? So how would you suggest we hurry things up?'

'I'm not absolutely sure yet, but I'd like to start with a hypothesis.'

'What hypothesis?'

'That these men have started their work again. They got scared when the film went missing, killed the two girls, then probably laid low for about three or four months. Then, once it was obvious the police believed the brunette had killed herself and the blonde had had an accident, they started moving again. Milan must be very lucrative, you'd start again, too, if you were in their place.'

'I'm not sure I like you associating me with that kind of work,' Carrua said: being in a hotel, he was trying hard not to shout. 'But yes, I'd start again.'

'If you start working again,' Duca went on, 'even though he was sure Carrua had already understood, 'you do the same things you did a year ago, the same things that proved to be very lucrative, that is, you go in search of new girls, who are only just entering the circuit, and you make them enter your circuit before the competition gets them. So we can start from that hypothesis: the men we're interested in are working again, here in Milan, even now, this evening.'

Carrua was motionless, as if turned to wood, that was how he was when he concentrated. 'All right, if we assume they are working again, we set the usual trap. We take a girl, send her out on the streets to do what the girls in the photographs were doing and at some point she'll be picked up by one of these men, and once we've caught one, we'll catch them all. It's worth a try. What do we have to lose?'

It might not work out like that. 'The girl could lose a lot. Who do you have in mind?'

'Mascaranti has a personal archive of women who could do it.'

'Think about it, Superintendent Carrua, you can't use a professional. These people are looking for fresh fruit, just plucked from the branch. You can't deceive them with a whore disguised as a semi-virgin. And I'm sorry if I said whore.'

'It's all right, don't get angry.'

'But I also have fresh fruit, just off the branch,' Mascaranti said, the phrase had the syntactic tone of a salesman offering the best merchandise.

'Mascaranti, you didn't have to say it,' Duca said, irritably but patiently: a doctor always knows how to keep his self-control. 'I know you have your informants even in good families, you even have them in clinics, among nurses, to keep an eye on the use of morphine and other pleasures, but try to understand the work that this fresh fruit of yours would have to do: let herself be approached by a whole lot of men before finding the one we're looking for, if she finds him. A girl who may be a virgin, who may have a boyfriend, won't do this work for you just to please the police.'

Silence. Then Carrua said, 'It seems to be raining,' he stood up and went to the window and saw the neon signs in the Piazza Cavour reflected in the wet street. 'Maybe you have the girl we need,' he said without turning; he realised that it was raining softly, gently, summer rain without a storm.

'Yes, if I were a criminal I would have one,' Duca said, also standing up. 'Maybe I am a criminal.' He went and sat down on the bed, picked up the phone and asked the switchboard for a number. 'Is it really raining?' he asked stupidly. The other two had also stood up, they suddenly seemed extremely interested in the rain, and they turned their backs on him and started looking out of the other window.

'Livia, please.' A man's voice had answered, a middle-aged man, he thought.

'Do you want to speak to Signorina Livia Ussaro?' the man said, stubbornly.

'Yes, signore, please.' It must be her father.

'Could you please tell me who's calling?' The fellow clearly believed in the formalities, phone calls from men must annoy him.

'Duca Lamberti.'

'Luca Lamberti?'

'No, Duca, D for Domodossola,' he was starting to get annoyed, too. He heard Livia's voice in the background: 'It's all right, dad,' then in the foreground, warm, with nothing at all frigid in it: 'I'm sorry, that was my dad.'

'I'm sorry, too.' How polite they both were. But was it really raining? 'I need to see you, immediately. Is that possible?'

'I've been waiting a long time for you to call.'

He wasn't being very honest, he was virtually pimping. 'I'll come and pick you up in ten minutes. OK?'

'Fine. I'll wait out front.'

He put the phone down and looked at the three men standing in the middle of the room. Was it really raining? Then he'd be able to take her to the Torre Branca, Milan's touching answer to the Eiffel Tower: in this weather there wouldn't be anybody there. He stood up. 'I should be able to tell you something tomorrow,' he said to Carrua.

'No, I'll tell you now,' Carrua said, as if letting fly at him. 'You're not to do anything. Drop it now, don't get mixed up in our work any more. I absolutely forbid it.'

'Why?' he asked, almost respectfully: he was from Emilia Romagna, he knew how to keep a cool head.

'Two girls have already been killed,' Carrua said: he was from Sardinia, red-blooded and calculating.

'I know that. I know it perfectly well.'

'You're a private citizen, not a policeman. A third woman's corpse is not in your remit. I caution you against taking any further interest in this case.'

'All right,' Duca said, already by the door. He had been cautioned, seriously cautioned, Carrua was not joking. 'Good night.'

'Duca, be careful.'

He went out without answering. They were right, but they didn't understand, they had to follow the law, and the law is strange sometimes, it favours criminals and ties honest men's hands.

It really was raining, and in less than ten minutes he had already picked up Livia from outside her building, and in less than twenty, with the Giulietta, they got to the Torre Branca, and in another three minutes they were in the round bar of the Torre, more than a hundred metres above the Po Valley and in particular over the complex of Sant'Ambrogio. It was raining harder than ever, the summer drizzle was turning into a storm, and through the windows, as if from a plane, they saw the sky turn bright with streaks of lightning. The portable radio which the barman had kept on was like a pan full of chestnuts exploding. An unused film set, perfect for the dirty business he had to talk to her about.

'Is it about Alberta that you wanted to see me again?' Livia asked.

'Yes.' She was wearing a dress with white flowers on a black background, large flowers, rather in the same style as the dress she had worn the other time, a small black straw handbag, her lips and nails painted pale orange, a large wristwatch, a man's watch, almost out of place with such a feminine dress. Particular signs: the way in which she looked at him, he wasn't being honest with her.

'Go on,' she said.

He told her everything, dotting the i's and crossing the t's, hoping she would then say no.

She didn't say either yes or no, instead she launched into what sounded as if it was going to be a long speech. He had to let her carry on, it was the only satisfaction he could give her, he had nothing to offer her but blood and tears, like Churchill.

'I haven't done any other experiments like that since Alberta died,' his Livia Ussaro said, while the thunder roared ever louder in the background. 'Her death was the ultimate evidence that private prostitution is impossible. I wrote in my notes that a woman is a piece of merchandise that's too much in demand, she represents a financial and social element that's too large for a whole structure of interests not to be created around her.'

Old ideas, but correct ones. Little Miss General Topics wasn't expounding any revolutionary theories, just presenting the facts.

'It isn't possible for a woman, especially nowadays, for her own reasons and of her own free will, to carry out such activities privately. Everything is structured to take a percentage from her, to "protect" her, to "organise" her. Two years ago, during my first experiments, a corset maker insisted on giving me some suspenders, she'd already understood and I pretended to accept, then she told me that she knew a gentleman who'd be able to offer me much bigger gifts. A parking warden had seen me get out of the car of one of these men and had also understood. He said, "Listen, you don't have to make so much effort looking for something, and besides, it isn't good to go around the streets by yourself. Let me handle it for you. There are lots of foreigners who ask me what they can do. You stay at home, and when there's something I'll phone you, isn't that better?" Of course, it would have been much better, but apart from the fact that he wanted half, it would have become a professional activity, whereas I wanted to see if it was possible to remain an amateur. It isn't possible. I got very scared once, and I don't scare easily. Without realising it, I'd stopped for a moment in the Via Visconti di Modrone. It was afternoon, I didn't know it was an allotted area, at least in the evening, I was careful never to go where the professionals were, but that time I made a mistake. Suddenly a man got off a moped, it couldn't have been any clearer who he was if he'd worn a sign around his neck with the word *pimp* on it. What he said, more or less, was this: "Don't think you can do as you like. Tell me who your friend is and I'll smash his face in." He wouldn't believe I didn't have a friend. "I see," he said, "your friend doesn't want you any more, that means you're free, if you want to come over to me, I'll be your friend." He wanted to force me to be part of his stable, but there were too many people about and I managed to get away. But I was really scared.'

Livia was obviously completely mad, and he really would be a criminal to take advantage of such lucid madness. But maybe she would say no. In the meantime the lightning was dancing around them, the barman interrupted them to say that he was scared of storms and would never again agree to work in a place like this.

'Basically these days there's only one form of semi-prostitution without pimping. They could be nice girls who have an elderly friend, some even have two, plus a boyfriend, if they have one. Or they could be women separated from their husbands who have to be helped by someone, and if this someone is of modest means, he helps them for a while, a few months, then they have to look for another. Some of these nice ladies have sewing machines at home, and they sew for their neighbours, their acquaintances, a few distant relatives. Every now and again someone comes to see them. "How are you, signora?" "Oh so-so," it may be a neighbour from where they lived before, or the pharmacist who gives them credit. "Don't be offended, signora, I brought you something." "Oh, you shouldn't have, I can't accept that." "It's only a handbag, it isn't a diamond ring." '

How well she imitated the voices, was this tower really solid? Go on talking, my darling, and then say no.

'In my opinion, that kind of prostitution is odious, because it's hypocritical. I'd never do anything like that.' She was talking, oh, yes.

She liked things to be clear and above board: really mad people didn't like shades of grey, compromises. Maybe the tower was very solid, but in any case the storm suddenly abated, the lightning stopped, the rain and thunder faded.

'I've talked too much, I know, when I'm with you I always talk too much, I just wanted to explain why I want to help you. I've done my experiments and I've understood where the evil lies, of course I do, they even debated it in parliament: it lies with the pimps. We'll never be able to eliminate it, but every time we find a pimp we have to crush him.' Passionately, she put both hands on the table. 'Tell me exactly what I have to do.'

Here she was, another apostle, crushing evil. Together, they were crusaders. She really believed she could crush it, but what exactly do you want to crush, my darling? The more of them you crush, the more there are. And that's all right, but maybe you have to crush them all the same.

'Think it over for a few days, before you agree.'

'You don't have to speak like that to me, I don't need to think it over, I'm a quick thinker.'

Yes, yes, darling. 'All right, then think of those two girls, they're both dead. If we get this wrong you could join them.'

'I've already thought about that.'

'And remember that we have everyone against us, even the police, and we won't be protected by anyone.'

'I've thought about that, too.'

'Well, then,' and now there was a solemnity in the way he spoke to her that was more intimate than ever, 'think about this. Every day you'll have to go with one or two men, for weeks, maybe to no avail, maybe we won't find anything, or maybe you'll be the third victim, but think about that seriously, we're not playing games here.' In his anger, he forgot himself and swore. 'I'm sorry,' he said.

Coldly, she said, 'You didn't have to say that to me. You've introduced a personal note into the question. From what you told me, and from the way you told it, it seems you don't like the idea of me having to go with men. If that's the case, it distorts everything, quite apart from the fact that I'm not remotely interested in what you like or don't like. You asked me to do this work, and as soon as I said yes, you said no. You're the one who's playing games, not me.'

Be quiet, be quiet, why did he always have to get into things he couldn't get out of, things that ended up as matters of life and death?

'Tell me what I have to do, and that's it. I'm old enough to know what I'm doing, if I'd wanted to say no I'd have said no. But I can't.'

She couldn't. 'All right, then let's go up on the terrace and get some fresh air, the rain has almost stopped.'

Up there, looking down at the lights of Milan, there was quite a wind: it was damp, like a wet sheet in the face. He explained to her the abominable details of the filthy work they had to do, he gave her the foul instructions that would make it less dangerous for her, he explained the signal: 'If you put your elbow out of the window once, that means "found him." If you put it out twice in a row that means "danger." Tomorrow, I'll bring Davide to see you and we'll do a rehearsal together, as soon as there's something that's not right, make the signal and he'll be there.' Because that was how it was, now he was even getting the other poor bastard involved. When someone was as sick in the head as he was, they didn't know any limits.

Then he took his Livia Ussaro and drove her home. At the front door they even shook hands, they might as well have said, 'Thanks for the company.' He went back to the Cavour feeling completely nauseated with everything, starting with himself, but not with her.

PART THREE

*'Maybe you never got beyond those girls in leather jackets standing
by the jukebox, those scrubbers from 1960 with their long hair all
straggly as if they'd drowned: according to you, they can streetwalk
in the Corso Buenos Aires at night, but nobody else. I think
you're behind the times.'*
*'That may be, I'd never thought of graduates in
history and philosophy doing it.'*

1

Here is Livia Ussaro at work, in the last stretch of the Via
Giuseppe Verdi, close to the Piazza della Scala, just after
half past ten. The area has been carefully chosen, like a rare
literary text, after a three-way meeting, with Davide as a lis-
tener but without a right to vote. She's neatly dressed, all in
blue, her skirt is short and under her little jacket she's wearing something so skimpy you couldn't really call it a blouse.
The impression she needs to give, as she walks up towards
the Piazza della Scala, is that she's looking for someone or
something, a shop perhaps, or is waiting for a date. And that
is indeed the impression she gives.

Davide has taken up position under the portico in the
Piazza della Scala, his Giulietta, thanks to a thousand-lire tip,
is parked by the monument to Leonardo da Vinci in such
a way that he can pull out easily. For many mornings now,

nothing has happened. Yes, there were two gentlemen who spoke to Livia, but one she ruled out because he didn't have a car—the person they want to meet definitely uses a car—the other because he was a young man of twenty-two or twenty-three, who had started by saying to her, 'Hey, good-looking!' and the person they're looking for is not a young man, he must be over fifty, and he certainly wouldn't use a phrase like 'Hey, good-looking!'

That morning, from under the arcade, Davide saw a tall man in his fifties walk up to Livia as she appeared to be waiting for the lights to turn green. Livia's conversation with the gentleman continued, rather than breaking off immediately like the others: obviously Livia had thought it was worth a try.

Indeed it was, and she crossed the Via Manzoni with the man, even smiling at him once, but in a very refined way. The very fact that Livia had accepted his company meant that the man had a car and that she had kindly consented to be given a lift. Davide walked to the Giulietta, now it was all a question of where the distinguished-looking street Casanova had parked his car, but Livia made it easier, slowing her suitor down until Davide was able to catch up with them.

It was all easy now: the man's car, a beautiful black Taunus, was also parked by the Leonardo monument, only it was stuck in the middle of the anthill and Davide had time to smoke almost a whole cigarette before the other man managed to get out and he was able to follow him. The route, too, had been carefully chosen: Via Manzoni, Via Palestro, Corso Venezia, Corso Buenos Aires, Piazzale Loreto. The reasons were twofold: Livia would tell her companion she had to go to the beginning of the Viale Monza, a long enough route to give her time to talk to him. If Livia judged that it was worth continuing, she would accept his gallant proposition and tell him to drive in the direction of Monza, where there were some fairly quiet spots. Otherwise, she would convince the man that she had made a mistake, that it was the first time she had accepted a lift and she would never do it again because men always tried to take advantage.

The Taunus followed the prearranged route under an increasingly hot sun, joined the compact river of vehicles streaming along the Corso Buenos Aires, reached the Piazzale Loreto, did a turn around the metro station, and stopped at the beginning of the Viale Monza. Davide, risking a fine, parked right behind them. He could see Livia and the man: the man seemed to be insisting, but Livia was shaking her head very sternly. The farce lasted a couple of minutes, then the gentleman resigned himself, got out, opened the door to his grouchy passenger, and helped her out, it was obvious he was still insisting, but Livia was unmoveable: virtue personified.

When the Taunus had left—another basic rule: take the number of all these men's cars, even when the encounter led nowhere, and he had taken this one—Livia waited for a while, then got into the Giulietta next to Davide.

'He's a madman,' Livia said, although with barely a smile, 'either that or it's the heat, he has business cards with him and gave me one. Look, give it to Duca.'

Armando Marnassi, exclusive representative for Alcheno food colouring, there followed two addresses and two telephone numbers. Davide put it in his jacket pocket, he would give it to Duca. 'Why's he mad?' he asked, driving towards the Via Plinio.

'He immediately offered me a job, two hundred thousand lire a month, he needs a trustworthy secretary. Then he told me he's invested his money in various apartments, and if I wasn't happy with the one where I'm living, he'd gladly give me one. If the journey had been longer and he didn't already have a wife, he might even have asked me to marry him.' If he hadn't given her his business card, she might have thought that all these offers were bait, but a man of that age who gives his name, address, and telephone number is clearly quite serious. Maybe he was one of the few older, but still youthful, men who didn't have a lady friend with an apartment or a boutique, and was trying to remedy the lack as quickly as possible.

In the afternoon, after a few hours' break, they started again. At half-past three Livia Ussaro was in the second area: from the Piazza San Babila to the Piazza San Carlo, making the round of the shopping arcades, apart from the area of the Via Montenapoleone—not because it was sexless, but because it was given over to other equally demanding activities. At that hour, especially in summer, mature men sleep, the most active in heavy armchairs, the spoiled actually in bed. Only at four-thirty or five do they return to their desks, discreetly sprinkled with rare and refreshing colognes, ready to make important decisions. But at the same time, many young women, from Milan or from out of town, often pretty, who don't need afternoon naps and are immune to the heat, wander that area looking in the windows, making a few purchases or meeting friends. If a middle-aged man interested in such things knows of this habit, he knows that it's at this time and in the areas richest in shops that he will find what interests him, so he gives up his own afternoon nap, and goes there. It's actually a discreet hour, with nothing dubious about it: a man over fifty in the company of a slim young brunette doesn't seem like a faun at that hour, but like her uncle. Assuming the person they were looking for still existed, and was still devoted to his activity, this was the area in which there was most likelihood of meeting him. That was why they combed the same area in the evening, too, from nine to ten-thirty, giving it the name Area 2b: it was the time when the cinemas and theatres were busy, they just had to keep away from the Corso Venezia, where the professionals worked, and concentrate a bit more on the Corso Matteotti, to have the best chance of having a few encounters.

The command post of this complex system is an apartment in the Piazza Leonardo da Vinci, Duca's apartment, bought by his father. On the door there's still a name plate saying *Doctor Duca Lamberti*, there used to be one by the street door which said *Duca Lamberti, doctor and surgeon*, which he had immediately removed, but as for the one on his apartment door, he had put a strip of tape over the word *Doctor*, and one morning found that someone had taken away the tape, the usual stupid delivery boy or local kid. He'd put on the strip again, but once again it was taken off, and he gave up.

Duca is in charge of the command post, he invented the

system down to its smallest details, and now he just has to wait for Davide's evening reports. Until after eleven at night, when Davide arrives, he has absolutely nothing to do except wait for the phone to ring, Livia Ussaro might spot the target at any moment, and then the phone would ring. But is it likely?

While he waits, he devotes himself to family life, to his sister Lorenza, to his niece Sara. After three years in prison, spending all this time at home—he can't leave because the phone call might come while he's out—he's discovered many things. He's discovered, for example, that his sister has become fearful. When he had seen her the last time before being arrested, she had seemed triumphant, triumphant with courage, almost as if his arrest and trial were an honour. She had written to him in prison that all the newspapers were talking about him, that he was becoming a famous doctor, that she was sure he would be acquitted and after it he would have thousands of patients, and very soon his own clinic.

Things were very different now. He was with her from the time when, together, they got up and took care of the child, together cleaned the house, made something to eat, and the fear was constant. She was afraid of everything. She had been so happy when he had come back and told her he'd be staying for a while, but one afternoon, in the kitchen, while Sara was asleep, he had had to tell her why, talk to her about Livia Ussaro and the two girls who had posed for photographs and then died, and their search for those responsible.

'Why are you doing it?' she had asked apprehensively.

It was hard to explain it to her, Lorenza wasn't like Livia

Ussaro who fed on abstract concepts. Lorenza needed facts, concrete concepts such as today is Monday and tomorrow is Tuesday. He replied, 'I was given the task of treating a young man, Davide, and was even being paid for it. Now what's wrong with Davide isn't so much that he drinks, but something else, something deeper: he has to learn to live again, to deal with his fellow men, and to teach him how to do that, I need to give him something to do. What he's doing now is a treatment on a large scale, which should certainly cure him: it's hunting for the man who killed Alberta. If he manages to find him, if he manages to catch him and punish him, he'll finally feel like a living, breathing man, and won't need to drink again. To him, Alberta was like his first love: he has to avenge her, and revenge both feeds and cures.' Maybe it was a bit too simplistic, but it was certainly concrete.

Lorenza had said nothing, but continued to be afraid. 'What if something happens to that girl? You were the one who made her do this work.'

Yes, he was in charge, and something could indeed happen to Livia Ussaro. But he was almost certain that nothing would happen to her, for the simple reason that she wouldn't find anyone or anything. The more time passed, the more often Davide arrived in the evening and reported that nothing had happened, the more far-fetched his plan seemed.

That evening, too, Davide called from the street and he threw down the front-door key. In the kitchen there was chilled beer waiting for him, but before drinking, he reported the few things that had happened during the day. Livia had accepted two rides that seemed likely, but in the

Viale Monza, as usual, she had got out: these were honest married men who had stayed in the city and were driving around in their cars, trying their luck, but without too much conviction.

In all these days of searching, Livia had come across everything, except what they were looking for. She had even found a lesbian and that had been extremely bothersome: the woman wouldn't let her go, she had followed her along the street, doing so much propaganda in favour of what she called parisexualism that, as Livia had confessed to him over the phone, she had had to make a certain effort to refute all these arguments. 'From a theoretical point of view, I assure you I was almost convinced, there are dialectically irreproachable reasons why parisexualism has the same rights as heterosexuality.' Even over the phone, she couldn't help indulging in her love of abstraction, and he let her talk: it was the only reward he could give her.

Everything had happened during these days, except what they were hoping would happen. Livia had even had to confront a violent drunk. She hadn't realised until she was already in his car, and had had to give the danger signal: twice she had put her arm out of the window and Davide had overtaken the drunk's car and boxed it in. Davide's bulk had convinced the drunk not to protest and Livia had been taken safely home. On another occasion, two police officers had approached Livia one evening in San Babila and asked her for her papers. The word *schoolteacher* on her identity card had reassured them somewhat: they were well-brought-up young men who respected culture and couldn't imagine that someone who had graduated in history and philosophy was streetwalking in San Babila, but they had advised her to go home anyway.

But Signor A had not appeared. They called him Signor A rather than Signor X, because the man wasn't an unknown quantity: he was something specific, the chief pimp. Duca didn't know his name or physical appearance, but he knew he existed. It's like when you say the fattest man in Milan: you've never seen him, you don't know if he's a chemist or a restaurant owner, if he's fair-haired or dark, but you know he exists, it's just a matter of finding him and weighing him, and then you'll immediately recognise him because he's the one who weighs more than anyone else in Milan. Of Signor A, though, there was still no sign.

'Davide, please give me your list of car registration numbers.' The transistor radio was playing dimly: Lorenza had left it on before going to bed. The good smell of warm concrete came up from the courtyard through the open window of the kitchen, the beer got warm even if you left it there for half a minute, you had to drink it immediately, which was what they did. He leafed through the notes that Davide had given him, there were exactly twenty-three car licence numbers, of which only four weren't from Milan, one of them was French.

Mascaranti, who was participating secretly in the operations, unknown to Carrua, had checked these numbers one by one but only to make absolutely sure: they already knew from Livia that these cars belonged to people who were not involved, a fact which Mascaranti had only confirmed. One by one, the owners of the cars had been checked, but Signor A wasn't one of them. Mascaranti had even found someone being sought by the police in Florence, and had had him arrested, but not Signor A.

How long would they have to go on with this search? Every evening, he was tempted to wind it up. Carrua could handle the case perfectly well, it was his job, and he'd have the help of Interpol. Why had he, Duca, got so worked up about it, what did it have to do with him anyway, and why had he got Livia Ussaro involved? But then he would put it off for another day.

He gave the useless list back to Davide. 'Have a whisky, then we can sleep.' He still had to give him a bit of whisky, Davide couldn't function only on beer. But he was a good boy, he didn't drink surreptitiously, even now when he could, because during the day, following Livia, he was free to enter any bar he wanted, and in the evening he went back to the Cavour to sleep by himself and he could drink whatever he liked. But he didn't.

In a small cupboard in the kitchen there were a couple of bottles of whisky, Davide took the one already opened, served himself copiously—Duca had ordered him to—and after drinking summed up his thoughts by saying, 'Why does it have to be a man in his fifties?' He waited in vain for a reply then said, 'Usually it's a young man, the type that women like, the type who can win them over.'

Duca switched off the transistor radio as it was starting to broadcast the latest political news. 'Those young men you mention don't take photographs, they work on damaged

181

goods, I'm sorry, I meant on women who don't have much and are all too ready to prostitute themselves, and they're all well known to the police. The person we're looking for does something very different, and on a larger scale. He looks for new girls, of a certain style, like Alberta, he probably has to supply high-class brothels in Italy and abroad. It's all highly organised, exactly like an import-export company. They need the photographs so that they can send them or take them personally to other people involved in the trade. All fifty photographs from a Minox roll can be fitted comfortably into an envelope or can be hidden in a packet of cigarettes, even a full one and from the negatives you can even make 30×45 enlargements. A lot of men are shy, they prefer to choose a woman by looking in a kind of album. Besides, keeping a dozen girls in an apartment is always dangerous, so instead they have the album, the man chooses, number 24 for example, and at the time and place arranged he'll find number 24. But for this traffic they don't need the usual girls who are already out there on the streets, the kind who'd listen to that nice young man of yours. And to win over this high-class merchandise, I'm sorry, I'm still talking about women, it takes a mature man, an expert. Think about Alberta, she would certainly never have let herself be persuaded by a young man with slicked-back hair just out of the hairdresser, it takes a mature man, someone who's confident, a gentleman, the kind of man who always makes an impression on women. Unlike me, you haven't been in prison for three years, so you're a bit lacking in technical knowledge. In prison I enjoyed, without wanting to, the friendship of a big procurer, who explained to me almost everything about his activity, that's why as soon as I saw those photographs alarm bells started ringing, and when we found out that the two women who had posed had been killed, I had the proof that this was a large organisation. Small-time pimps don't kill, or very seldom, but in a vast organisation you have to be ruthless.'

This crash course on prostitution continued for a while, until they were interrupted by little Sara crying in the next room.

'It's nearly one,' he said to Davide, 'at one she drinks two hundred grams of milk with her eyes closed, almost without waking up, has a pee at the same time, and then she's out like a light until tomorrow morning at six or seven. I've always thought that kind of vegetable life is the most civilised. I think civilisation ends, at least for the human race, as soon as brain activity starts.'

This second crash course, on social metaphysics, was also interrupted: by the ringing of the telephone.

He stood up, anxiously. He often sensed things before they happened, oh yes, he was a magician. He smiled at Davide and went into the hall. There was a tranquil smell of wax and gas.

'Hello?'

He heard Livia's voice. 'I've found him.'

2

You didn't need to be a mind reader to understand who she had found: Signor A.

'But didn't Davide take you home?' he asked. At eleven o'clock Davide had indeed taken her home, not driving away until he had seen her go inside the building and close the street door behind her. Where had she found Signor A? On the landing outside her apartment?

'Yes,' his Livia said in her beautiful, limpid voice, 'but then I had to go out again almost immediately.'

'Why?'

'Dad wasn't feeling well, he had a terrible toothache and there was nothing in the apartment to ease the pain, so I had to go out to the pharmacy.'

'I see.'

'There weren't any taxis, at that hour they're all parked outside the cinemas. I walked to the Piazza Oberdan, where there's an all-night pharmacy.'

'That's quite a distance from your apartment.'

'I had no choice. There was only one other customer in the pharmacy, a man. When I saw him, it struck me he was exactly the kind of man we were looking for. I bought a tube of painkillers and left.'

Livia Ussaro even did overtime. She had worked until eleven with Davide, then had seen an interesting man, and had carried on working.

'He followed me.' She had done nothing to make him follow her, she had been only the innocent prey, she had given him the impression that she was what he was looking for.

'Tell me everything.'

'Outside the pharmacy, I stopped at the curb to let the cars pass. Then he said that everyone was getting headaches in this heat.'

'What did you do?'

'I didn't reply, just smiled a little, but as if I was annoyed.'

Perfect. Then his Livia Ussaro had crossed the Corso Buenos Aires to where the taxi stand was. Obviously, the stand was empty, you never see a taxi stand with lots of taxis, except when you don't need them. Signor A had tactfully followed her, without saying another word, as if he wasn't following her, as if he had also had to cross the street, but when he had seen her stop at the taxi stand, he must have thought he was a lucky man.

'I'm afraid you'll have a long wait,' he had said.

Another smile from her, without words, but less annoyed, more words from Signor A, and finally she had followed him, accepting the lift he had so politely offered her, and had got into Signor A's dark blue Flaminia.

'The number, Livia.' The licence number. Even if it had been a twenty-figure number, she was sure to remember it, without needing to write it down.

'Duca, maybe I'm stupid, but I didn't catch it.' She sounded as if she wanted to cry.

She hadn't caught the licence number, his ace of spies had failed in the simplest of operations. 'How can that be?'

'Duca, cars have number plates on the front and the back, but when you get in, you get in from the side, where there are no number plates,' she excused herself timidly, without hope, as if knowing she had already been condemned. 'All the time I was with him, I tried to find an opportunity to look at the number, but it wasn't possible, he kept me inside the car, I couldn't get out and look at the number plate without making him suspicious, I couldn't, I really couldn't.'

He wasn't going to let her off that easily. 'But when he left you and drove off, you could have seen the number plate at the back as the car was leaving.'

'No, I couldn't do that either. He insisted on driving me all the way back to the front door of my building, and he waited until I'd gone inside, I don't know if he did it only out of gallantry, but I had to close the door behind me after going in, I opened it again as soon as I heard him leave, but the car was already some distance away and the street isn't very well lit.'

It happens. The great chef calmly cooks venison *all'imperiale* with California oranges soaked in rum, and then messes up a scrambled egg.

'So what *do* you know about him?' he asked, almost roughly.

'The photographs.'

Signor A had taken his Livia towards the Parco Lambro, not precisely into the park, which at that hour would have been a little dangerous, but into a quiet avenue next to it, and besides, for what he had to do, he could have parked in the Piazza del Duomo at midday, because he hadn't

A Private Venus

done anything except talk, although it was quite an erotic conversation. He had asked her a lot of questions, but discreet ones: how old was she, what region was she from, did she have a boyfriend? He'd been pleased to hear that she was a schoolteacher, even though she wasn't teaching at the moment, he said that culture in a woman was the thing that excited him the most. He had indulged in a few weary caresses, then had confessed sincerely that at his age, inevitably, things changed in your body, things you couldn't do much about. Of course if he was twenty, he had said with a smile, everything would have been different, but now he only came alive when he saw photographs of beautiful women, obviously with not too many clothes on, in fact, with no clothes at all, she had to understand his plight, a photographic nude had more effect on him than a real nude, especially if he had met the girl in the photograph and talked to her a bit, nude photographs in the specialised magazines left him indifferent, because he had never met the women in them; he would have liked, for example, to have a nice series of photographs of her, now that he had spoken to her and seen what a nice, attractive person she was. Of course, she didn't have any photographs like that, but this was a small inconvenience which could immediately be remedied. He had a friend, a completely trustworthy friend and an expert photographer, that she could go and see. As an expression of his gratitude, he would be happy if she would accept fifty thousand lire, and last but not least he had reassured her that nobody would ever know about it, she would pose with her face in shadow, and anyway it was in his interest to keep this

187

weakness of his a secret. Livia had told him she didn't like the idea, she didn't even like what she was doing with him now, and she didn't want to do it any more even though her financial situation was difficult. Signor A had praised her for this stand of hers and had even expressed the fervent hope that she would find a good job and then a nice young man and get married, but a few photographs wouldn't make any difference, would they?

He had insisted, subtly, and in the end he had given her the address of his friend the photographer, even adding an extra twenty thousand lire.

'Tell me the address,' Duca asked his Livia Ussaro impatiently. He had signalled to Davide, who he could see through the open door of the kitchen, to come and write.

'Publicity Photographic,' Livia said.

'Publicity Photographic,' he repeated and Davide wrote it down.

'Ulisse Apartments, beyond the Via Egidio Folli and beyond the tollbooth,' Livia said.

'Ulisse Apartments, beyond the Via Egidio Folli and beyond the toll booth,' he repeated and Davide wrote it down. 'And when do you have to go?'

'He told me to be there between two and three in the afternoon, because after that his friend has some work to do outside the studio.'

It was a well-chosen time, Milan would be asleep at home, Milan overwhelmed by the heat but unable to sleep in the streets, on the trams, in offices, in factories: it was a more solitary and discreet time than any hour of the night.

'And now the description,' Duca said, signalling to Davide again to make sure he wrote everything down. 'Height?'

'At least one metre seventy-five, he's taller than me and I'm one metre seventy,' she said, adding innocently, 'in high heels.'

'Height one metre seventy-five. Build?'

'Thin, his jacket hung on him.'

'Complexion?'

'A bit olive. He has a moustache, very thin, grey, almost white.'

'Hair?'

'Also grey, almost white, with a receding hairline, but he still has a lot of hair and he wears it quite long and well combed.'

'Eyes?'

Livia hesitated. 'I'm sorry, I didn't catch the colour.'

'Nose?'

'A bit aquiline, but only a bit.'

It wasn't much, but he'd pass this information on to Mascaranti, who would have an identikit made by the police draughtsmen. His hope lay in the photographer: if they managed to get him he would give them the name of his accomplices, including Signor A. They had a better chance to catch him now.

'Livia.'

'Yes.'

'Listen carefully to what I'm going to tell you.'

'Yes.'

'Stay at home until I tell you otherwise.'

'Yes.'

'Never answer the phone personally. If they call, get a member of your family to answer, and have them say you're not there.'

'Yes.'

'Never open the door yourself, send someone, and if they ask for you, same answer, you're not there.'

'Yes.'

'Obviously nobody will come tonight, but from tomorrow morning at six, I'll phone you every hour to make sure nothing has happened.'

'What could happen?'

'I don't think anything will, but after what happened last year they may have become more cautious. They may be watching you to see if you have contacts with anyone.' That wasn't the only thing, but he didn't tell her the rest. 'Now go to bed, Livia. And thank you.'

'I'm so glad I succeeded,' she said, her girlish voice triumphant.

Only when he put down the receiver did he notice that Lorenza was standing in the square, bare, yet intimate hall, her eyes cloudy with fear.

'Go to bed, don't worry.'

'Who was it?' She couldn't help worrying, she knew everything, Duca had told her everything, and it was a horrible business.

'Livia. We found the man.'

'What are you going to do now?'

He became nervous because he felt sorry, eaten up with remorse, because she was right: it was stupid, criminal, that instead of looking for a good job he should get involved in this disgusting affair. 'Maybe I'll go out, maybe I'll stay here, but there's one thing I'd like, which is for you to go to bed without worrying about me.'

Lorenza turned red, because of that tone, and because Davide was there, listening, she looked at him, she seemed to be about to say something, but she was dominated by her big brother, and she went back to her room.

'A guide to Milan,' he said to Davide. They went into the living room, which was a little larger than the hall, and where among the other so-called furniture in the so-called Rational style—chosen by his father, who had thought he would like it—there was a small bookcase with books and old magazines, the beginnings of a library that had remained unfinished when he had gone into prison, three years earlier. There was also dust, because Sara didn't give her mother much time to see to the house, and there was also a guide to Milan, a little book with a nice map, a bit out of date, but it might still be useful. They went back in the kitchen, laid the map out on the table, looked at the list of streets: Via Egidio Folli, at the very edge of the city, just behind the Parco Lambro, the street then joined the main road that led to Melzo and Pioltello. 'They've become very cautious,' he said.

'Why?' Davide asked.

'They're not confident enough these days to set up their studio in the middle of town. They've moved out of the centre, just like the big companies. At the first sign of anything going wrong, they can jump in their car and they're already on the main road.'

'What do we do now?'

'I'm thinking about that.' But it wasn't true, in broad terms he had already made up his mind, he was only pretending to think in order to convince himself that he wasn't working from a whim. It was all a lie.

If he had been an honest citizen, at this point he should have phoned Carrua, given him the information about the photographer, and let him deal with it. But he couldn't be an honest citizen, his criminal record showed that.

'How strange,' he said, 'if Livia Ussaro's father hadn't had a toothache, Livia wouldn't have gone out to the pharmacy and maybe we'd never have found anything with our system.'

'We have to do something,' Davide said: he was an impatient man and didn't realise he was basically saying the same thing for the second time.

'Of course,' Duca replied. 'Can you ride a bicycle?'

'I think so.'

'All right, now let's see what time the sun rises.' He had a diary, a very wonderful one, there were many wonderful things in it, including the fact that this week the sun rose at 5:32. 'That means that by five there's already a bit of light, so you have to leave here at 4:30.'

'And where do I have to go?' Davide asked.

'To the end of the Via Egidio Folli, to see where these Ulisse Apartments are, what they are, how far they are. If I went there by car I'd arouse suspicion.

'And the bicycle?'

'The caretaker's son has one. I'll wake the caretaker and ask him to let me borrow it, he'll be a bit surprised, but he likes me, I really don't know why.' It was the dead of night, and there was complete silence in the kitchen, as if everyone was asleep, and even the things in it seemed to be asleep—the empty beer bottles, the whisky bottle about to become empty, Sara's dummies and feeding bottles on a towel on the draining board by the sink—though he was sure Lorenza wasn't asleep. But even Lorenza couldn't understand.

'And afterwards?' Davide asked.

'You see, Davide,' he said, 'if they've become so cautious, we have to be cautious, too. Let me explain what we're going to do tomorrow. Just before two o'clock, Livia will call a taxi and go to this Publicity Photographic place. We'll follow her. But let's suppose that someone else, very cautiously, is also following Livia, to make sure that Livia doesn't have any friends with her, like us. If that's the case, this person will notice that we're following Livia, and then we won't get anywhere. Are you with me?'

'Of course,' Davide told him with his eyes.

'So we have to follow Livia, but indirectly. In other words, we'll go ahead of her, we'll set off a hundred metres in front of her and keep the same distance. But even then, only up to a certain point. Imagine the formation: first us, in the Giulietta, then the taxi with Livia and then, possibly, this person following Livia. While we're in the city, in the traffic, we can maintain this formation because the man won't notice that we're with Livia, given that we're in front of her, but by the time we get to the end of the Via Egidio Folli, we'll be on a road in the open country or almost,' he pointed at all the green on the map, 'and we'll probably be the only cars around at that hour. Then he may suspect, because we'll be all too visible. In addition, when we've got to these Ulisse Apartments, we'll have to park the car, if we park it right in front, we're rather naïve as pursuers. So you understand what you have to do there on the bicycle.'

He was starting to understand.

'You do a reconnaissance. After seeing exactly where the Ulisse Apartments are, you have to find two things for me: a place where we can hide the car as close as possible to the building and to the main road, but without it being visible from the building itself. And the other thing is a secondary street which is near the building but isn't the Via Folli. Or at least you have to be able to tell me if there's neither a spot to park nor a secondary road.'

Silence. They hadn't heard the whoosh of car tyres for about ten minutes. It was almost two in the morning, they still had many hours to wait, and they were not the kind of men to sleep on the night before a battle.

'My father liked playing solitaire,' he said to Davide. 'He must have left a few packs of cards here. Do you know how to play *scopa*?'

'Yes.' *Scopa* wasn't much fun with only two players, but they had to do something.

3

Livia emerged from the front door of her building and got into the taxi. It was just after 1:30, the traffic was starting to thin out: many people preferred to eat at that hour. 'Via Egidio Folli,' she said to the driver.

In the mirror she saw the driver giving the usual disgusted grimace: whatever address you give a taxi driver, he'll think it's a stupid destination. Why does anyone need to go to the Via Egidio Folli in their lives? Or to the Via Borgogna, for that matter? And maybe he was right.

The driver continued along the Via Plinio, crossed the Via Eustachi, the Viale Abruzzi, turned into the Via Nöe and reached the Via Pacini. At this point Livia admired Davide's driving skills, with which, of course, she was already famil-iar: the Giulietta with Davide and Signor Lamberti on board was ahead, always within sight, but never right in front of the taxi. Following a car by keeping ahead of it was a delicate operation in city traffic and Davide was performing perfectly.

Despite the heat and the nervous tension which flus-tered her a little, Livia noticed another thing: her taxi was being followed. There was no skill in this discovery: she had noticed the car immediately in the Via Plinio because it had left at the same time as her taxi, and because it was a lovely car, a Mercedes 230, of a colour she liked, a bronze which verged on greyish brown, like caffè latte. She had seen it again in the Via Nöe, then in the Piazzale Pola and now in the Via Pacini. The little mirror she had in her hand as she painted her lips every now and again told her how faithfully the Mercedes was following her taxi and also how unconcerned its driver seemed about being spotted.

The oral instruction manual she had been given by Signor Lamberti had covered that eventuality: 'If you notice you're being followed, ask the taxi driver to pull up at a news stand and buy a paper.' This simple operation would tell Signor Lamberti that she had a friend behind her.

'Could you stop at the next news stand, please?' she said to the driver who, resigned by now, made no grimace, but stopped the car in front of the news stand at the corner of the Via Teodosio. Livia got out and was pleased to see the Mercedes stop a little further on. She was much less pleased to see the Giulietta disappear quickly at the end of the Via Teodosio. She knew Signor Lamberti and Davide were still protecting her, but no longer seeing their car unsettled her. She bought a fashion magazine and immediately got back in the car.

In the Via Porpora, the driver asked, 'What number in the Via Folli?'

'At the end, just after the tollbooth.'

The driver shook his head. 'Then you'll have to pay my return fare.'

'Of course, don't worry.' Without ever turning her head to look back, using only her little mirror, she could still see the Mercedes perfectly well, it was just behind them now, gleaming in the sun, bronze, slender, and malign.

'The Via Folli ends here, we're in the countryside,' the driver said. 'Where is it I have to go?' The stupidity of passengers had made him brutish: they never even knew where they wanted to go.

'A bit further on, there's a large building on the left.' The road was running between cultivated fields and for a long stretch there were no houses of any kind: the illusion of being in open country was almost perfect.

'That one there?' the driver asked with a martyred air.

They could see it already. Signor Lamberti had described the street and the Ulisse Apartments to her over the phone, just as Davide had described them to him after going there by bicycle.

'Yes, that's the one.' She glanced in the little mirror, she could still see the Mercedes behind her. She wasn't afraid any more, she knew Signor Lamberti and Davide were close, closer than ever. Next to the sky-grey building which rose in the middle of the cultivated fields, all by itself, because of some clever bit of property speculation, there was an old farmhouse, more than a hundred metres from the main road, peeping out from a small wood, and that was where the Giulietta was, amid the greenery, in the open air but invisible, and that was where her friends were, also in the open air in the scorching heat of the hour, equipped with a modest but useful little telescope with which they could enjoy a view of the whole Ulisse building, with all its twelve floors and a little of the countryside around, so green and sunny, and yet so disturbing.

'This one?' the driver said as he stopped, even though there couldn't be any doubt: it was the only building amid all the fields, a twelve-storey sky-grey tower, gigantic and futuristic, vaguely reminiscent, in its isolation, of those monumental Aztec temples that emerge here and there in the wilderness. It was a building intended for human habitation, but nobody, or almost nobody, was living in it yet, even though all the apartments were already sold: people need to invest their money, they don't want to keep their money in the mattress like their grandparents, so it was complete, finished, equipped with every facility. Around it there was a large concrete parking area, with white lines to demarcate the parking spaces, only the cars were missing.

'Yes, this one,' Livia said. She got out and gave him a five-thousand-lire note, she took the change, leaving him a lot of coins, all the while looking around without turning her head, but the Mercedes had stopped a long way back, almost at the bend. It was a perverse kind of discretion.

The Ulisse Apartments did not have a caretaker. There was a large directory with buttons to press, and behind each transparent square was the name of the occupant. Livia pressed the one that had the words *Publicity Photographic* on it and almost immediately she heard the Entryphone crackle.

'Come right up, second floor,' a colourless voice said, and the crackling stopped. The glass gate opened with a click and at that moment Livia Ussaro felt like a fox putting its paw in a trap.

On the second floor, a young man in a white smock admitted her without saying a word and pointed to an internal door, and she found herself in the usual square room you found in so many apartments. The shutters on the two windows were hermetically sealed, and so were the windows, but there was air conditioning, and it felt all right. You couldn't say that the room was furnished. In a corner there were three standing lamps, off at the moment, in front of a much enlarged photograph of a high, decorative wave of the sea, presumably used as a background. In the opposite corner there was a big tripod with a kind of cigarette lighter on the top of it: Signor Lamberti had explained to her that this was the Minox. On a chair, the last and final piece of furniture in the room, there were some small-format magazines, and on top of them there was a chessboard, and on the chessboard a box with pieces, a black knight protruded from the box like a horse's head from a stall in a stable.

The first thing the young man in the white smock said was, 'You can get undressed in the bathroom, if you want.'

Although Livia was looking at him closely, she realised she wouldn't be able to describe the man, or his voice: it struck her that it would be like trying to describe the contents of an empty box.

'Yes, thank you,' she said, but she didn't move, she was clutching her handbag and fashion magazine to her dark red cotton dress.

'What's the matter?' he asked.

'They told me I'd be paid,' she said, politely but firmly.

'Yes, of course, but let's do the photographs first.'

'I'm sorry, we can do the photographs afterwards.' This was one of the instructions in Signor Lamberti's oral manual. The aim of it was to remove any lingering suspicion, if there was any: a girl who wants the money first is someone who cares only about herself and isn't playing a double game.

The young man in the white smock didn't smile, didn't say anything, simply left the room, and came back almost immediately with five ten-thousand-lire notes which he handed over to her in silence.

Livia took them and went into the bathroom. She undressed in a flash, without even closing the door. It was obvious the place had almost never been used, there were no toiletries, not even soap, just two brightly-coloured towels. As she left the bathroom she heard the young man swear, and from the way in which he uttered the swear word, a very vulgar one, she realised immediately, beyond any doubt, what he was: a homosexual, some ghastly new species. She thought that explained the colourlessness of his physical person, she thought it was like the monstrous colourlessness of the mutants described in science-fiction novels, exactly halfway through their mutation, when they still have the outer wrapping of humanity but their minds and nervous systems already belong to some ghastly new species.

'What happened?' she asked, conspiratorially, but politely.

'It keeps flashing,' the photographer said. In his hands he had one of the black leads from the lamps, it was broken and the plug was on the floor. 'I have to fix it.'

He hadn't looked at her even for a moment: she would have liked to know what a homosexual thinks about the female nude. She saw him go out, he was away for a few minutes, then he came back with some Scotch tape and a pair of scissors, and standing there he started adjusting the lead, which had come away from the plug just as he had been inserting it in the socket. Standing by the chair, she watched him in silence, then she remembered that the manual had ordered her to make conversation, a woman who doesn't talk is a woman who arouses suspicion.

'Do you play chess?' she said.

'By myself,' he replied. The mere word chess must have opened the secret doors of what, reluctantly, referring to such an individual, had to be called his soul. 'Almost nobody plays it these days.'

'I study the championship games, or I play with my father.' It was true, or almost, not that she spent her days playing chess, but that her father had taught her the game when she was a teenager, and chess was very congenial to her character. She saw the young man raise his head for a moment and look at her, not as a naked woman, but as an entity that understood chess. But he didn't say anything. So she continued, because it's useful to show your adversary that you share the same passions, 'Just a few days ago I saw a beautiful three-knight game in *Le Monde*.'

'It wasn't three days ago, it was more than a month ago, it was the game where Neukirch from Leipzig played white and Zinn from Berlin black.'

'Yes, that's the one, my father takes *Le Monde* because there's a chess section, and he keeps every issue, it may well have been a month ago, I played it last Monday or Tuesday.'

'I also take *Le Monde* for the chess section.' As he fixed the lead, he seemed to be pondering whether he should suggest to her that they play a game of chess.

'Do you remember the endgame? Black has had to move his king, then white moves his knight, threatening the bishop, black is forced to protect himself with the rook, but then white pushes the pawn forward and there's nothing more to be done, the next move is checkmate.'

'Yes, I remember very well,' and again he raised his head, a hint of joy in his eyes, almost that of the classical music lover who suddenly hears his favourite piece being played, and at the same time surprise that a woman should know so much about the magical world of chess. 'But I don't like knight games, they're too restricting.'

'Too cautious,' she replied, 'but they say it's only on the surface, at a certain point there's always a battle in the middle of the chessboard . . .' she said a few more phrases to complete the idea, but she had to control herself because she felt like laughing: here they were, a naked woman in a room with a homosexual fixing a lead, and they were talking about chess.

'Just a moment, please,' the photographer said. He had finished fixing the lead, but then something else had happened: they had heard the dull sound of a bell. The man dropped the wire on the floor, left the room, closed the door and in the hall picked up the Entryphone and lifted it to his ear.

'Open up,' a voice said.

So he pressed the button that opened the front door downstairs and waited, after a minute the door opened and in the corridor he saw the man get out of the lift, in a very light hazel-coloured suit, a shade of hazel just a little lighter than his hair. He closed the door behind him.

'How's it going?' the man asked. He, too, was young, but

there was an air of suppressed violence about him that made him seem less youthful than the photographer.

'I don't like her,' the first man said.

'Why?' The man spoke very quietly and very aggressively.

'I don't know, I just don't like her.'

'I never saw anyone. She came straight here without talking to anyone.'

'I still don't like her.'

'There must be a reason.'

'I don't know. She wanted the money first.' The photographer was whining a little now.

'Strange, I wouldn't have thought it. Sol said she was quite refined.' He was starting to have his suspicions now, too.

'Plus, she plays chess, like the one last year,' the man said, confessing the real reason. The previous year, that damned brunette had tricked him to such an extent that they had had to move everyone out, all because of his weakness for chess. And now this one here was also an expert on chess, and had been about to charm him, she even remembered the Neukirch game, but at the same time she had made him suspicious, where did all these female chess champions come from, when most people today only knew how to do the football pools or collect the prize figurines in boxes of detergents and cheese?

'I'll take a look.'

When they entered the room, Livia was in the corner, where the big photograph of the sea wave was, as if she was looking at the floodlights, but it was only so that she could be closer to the door and hear what was happening in the hall, although she hadn't been able to hear anything. She was pleased to see this other man, almost young, probably a little short-sighted. He was another of them, they would both be caught in the trap, but she pretended to be nervous. 'I didn't know there'd be anybody watching,' she said, 'I don't want anyone here apart from the photographer.'

'Of course, you're right, I'm going now,' the man said in a gentle voice, 'but first I'd like to ask you a few questions.' With his hand he swept away, not gently at all, everything that was on the chair, chessboard, chess pieces, magazines, and sat down.

'You're drunk, I've never seen you before and I have no desire to answer questions from a drunk.'

'But you're going to answer, because you're a nice person. Luigi, get a chair for the young lady.' He turned back to her as the other man went out. 'I've been told some nice things about you, I hear you're a graduate. Is that true?'

'Yes.' The most important instruction Signor Lamberti had given her was not to cause trouble, to make sure that everything happened simply and calmly. If she insisted on not wanting to answer, it would be dangerous.

'A graduate in what?'

The photographer came back in with the chair, but she gestured, no, she would never put her private parts on anything belonging to these people, even though it wasn't very pleasant standing there naked in front of the two of them. 'History and philosophy.'

'Do you teach?'

'No, I'm just a graduate.'

'And how do you live?'

'I do translations.'

'From what language?'

'I prefer to translate from English, but I can also translate from German and French.'

'Do these translations pay well?'

'Not really.'

'In other words, not enough to live on.'

'No. Otherwise I wouldn't be here.'

A pallid smile from the man. 'That's true. What does your father do?'

The mention of her father, in this place, in this situation, so exposed to the fortunately not lustful looks of the two men, hurt her like a whiplash, but she restrained herself. It was obvious that they suspected her, and she had to convince them they were wrong. 'He's a watchmaker, he repairs watches, especially antique ones,' she said calmly.

'He must have spent a lot of money on you, you with a degree and all.'

'I think he did.'

The man touched his right earlobe. 'But what I don't understand is how a person with your class would want to do something like this.' He seemed to be just chatting, as if in a fashionable drawing-room, so that it didn't seem like the brutal interrogation it was. 'I mean, you come from an honest family, your father has made sacrifices to let you study, you're cultured and have a good education, you know four languages, you translate books that are probably difficult, I've even heard you're an expert chess player. Don't you find it strange that, for a bit of money, a woman like you ends up streetwalking late at night in the Corso Buenos Aires?'

Perhaps the moment had come, as defenceless, exposed and dispirited as she was, to bring him up to date. 'Maybe you never got beyond those girls in leather jackets standing by the jukebox, those scrubbers from 1960 with their long hair all straggly as if they'd drowned: according to you, they can streetwalk in the Corso Buenos Aires at night, but nobody else. I think you're behind the times.'

Another vague smile from the man. 'That may be, I'd never thought of graduates in history and philosophy doing it. And frankly, graduates in history and philosophy who supplement their incomes with this kind of work make me suspicious.'

His tone, however polite, was very threatening. Livia shrugged. 'I don't know what to do about that,' she said. 'If you've finished your interrogation, I'd like to do those photographs and leave.'

'Yes, you're right. Luigi, switch on the floodlights and start.' He turned to her again. 'Signorina, where did you put your handbag?'

'Why?'

'Because when I have my suspicions, I like to check.'

'You can't look in my handbag,' she burst out, but only because she had to burst out, it was part of the play-acting.

'Oh, but I think I can,' he replied, getting to his feet. 'Where's that bag?'

'It's in the bathroom, go on, look in it, take the money if you want, I should have known I was dealing with crooks.'

'Yes, you're right, you should have told yourself we didn't come from a church youth club. But if you pose for the photographs, I won't take your money. Luigi, start,' and he went into the bathroom. The red canvas handbag was in full sight on the little shelf over the washbasin, he took out the money, there was the fifty thousand she had been given by the man called Luigi, plus a couple of thousand-lire notes and about a dozen five-hundred-lire coins. There was the usual lipstick, the usual mirror, the usual key ring with just two keys, the driving licence, a tiny, spotless handkerchief, folded into a triangle, and finally there was a really tiny address book, a woman's, filled neatly, in a microscopic but very clear handwriting. It was the only slightly battered object, the cover was a bit worn, it must be a few years old.

And nothing else. He put his head out of the door of the bathroom that gave on the room adapted as a studio. He could see the photographer moving around behind his Minox—'Move, there, stop, six, move, there, stop, seven, move, there, stop, eight'—but he couldn't see Livia. There was still time before they got to fifty photographs. He put everything back in the handbag, except the address book, and from his breast pocket he took out a pair of very normal glasses with tortoiseshell frames, which made him look like the model of a young cool jazz lover and started to read. At first he leafed through, just to get an idea of what kind of addresses the graduate kept, then he thought that he would proceed more methodically and started to read from the letter *A*. None of the names meant anything to him, but under *E* he found the addresses of three publishing houses,

Editions This and Editions That, so the girl really did translate. Under the letter *I* he found the address of an Institute of Italian-English culture, under the letter *M* that of a neo-anarchist movement which gave him pause for thought, was the girl an anarchist? Then at the letter *R* he found that name.

The photographer had been right to smell a rat. He went back in the room, sat down again, turning his back on Livia a little. They were on the thirty-ninth photograph, there were still a dozen to do, but he said to Luigi, 'That's enough now.' And to her, 'Come here, please, I have some more questions to ask you.'

'I'd like to get dressed,' she said. She was sure now that he had discovered something and that the battle was starting, she wasn't afraid, she only wanted to know what he could possibly have discovered in the handbag. The answer wasn't long in coming.

'Come here now, you bitch, or I'll break your legs, and tell me how you happen to know Alberta Radelli.'

So that was what he had discovered, but how could she have remembered that Alberta's name was still in her old address book? Things were turning difficult now, and she liked difficulty. She immediately obeyed and went and sat down in front of him, with the photographer watching her from behind, but she obeyed with the air of someone who's dealing with a madman.

'She was a friend of mine.'

'What do you mean, "was"? Did you quarrel?' He was setting a trap, trying to get her to lie.

'No, the poor girl died, she killed herself.' She didn't rise to the bait. All her intelligence was lit up like an electronic calculator, ready to fight the enemy's wiles.

'When?'

'A year ago.'

'How?'

'She slit her wrists. It was in all the papers.'

'Were you good friends?'

'Quite good.'

'Was she someone who went on the streets every now and again, like you?'

He thought he was being clever, in his way he was, he was just waiting for her to tell a lie, in order to jump on her. 'Yes. Maybe that's why we became friends.'

For a while the almost young man looked at her, he seemed more interested in her breasts then in her face, while he thought about his next move. Then he said to the photographer, 'Give me a roll of film.'

Luigi had a box of them in the pocket of his smock and immediately gave him one.

'Have you ever seen a roll of film like this?' And he again looked her in the eyes, his own eyes half closed, as if to focus better.

'Yes, it's a Minox cartridge.'

'And where have you seen one before?'

'It was at university, a friend of mine had a Minox.'

'Could other people have also showed you a roll like this?

'I don't remember. It's possible, maybe a photographer.'

'What about your friend Alberta? Didn't she ever show you one of these cartridges?'

'No.'

'Are you sure?'

'Yes.'

'And didn't your friend ever tell you that she'd been asked to pose for photographs like the ones you've just been doing?'

The lie had to be ready instantaneously in order to seem convincing. 'No.'

'Let's think about it: you and she are very good friends, you tell each other everything, even how much you earn from your streetwalking, and then she doesn't tell you she posed for some artistic photographs, or that she's about to. Strange.'

'We were good friends but we didn't see each other often, sometimes a month or two went by without our meeting.' She was starting to feel cold, but only because of the air conditioning on her naked skin, not because of anything else.

For a while the man remained silent, with his head down, he was looking at her feet, counting the toes, almost as if he was anxious to know how many there were altogether, to help himself to think. Then, still with his head down, he said, 'You're not telling us the truth. I think you know something. Maybe you know a lot.'

'But I don't even know what it is you want from me, I only know I've ended up in a den of thieves. Let me get dressed and go, you can keep the money if you like, but I want to leave.' She was playing her part almost perfectly.

'Luigi,' the man said, 'bring me the cotton wool and the alcohol, and also the peroxide.'

'I don't know if I have any peroxide.'

'Don't worry, it's just to stop the bleeding.' The man took out his glasses and put them on. At last he looked at her. 'If you tell me the whole truth, I won't do anything to you.' He also took out a penknife from one of his pockets, a modest, old-fashioned penknife, the kind that not even primary schoolchildren used any more.

'You're crazy! What do you want me to tell you? Try to touch me and you'll see what I can do.' She was playing the ingénue, maybe successfully.

'I'm not curious to know what you can do, but try to tell the truth and you'll see you won't have to do anything.'

Luigi reappeared with some small bottles in his hand. 'I found peroxide after all.'

The man took the bottles and put them on the floor by his feet. 'You still have time to tell me everything you know.'

She had never studied acting, but she tried to do the best she could, to scream at the top of her voice, a scream was the natural reaction of a terrified woman who didn't know anything. In reality, she knew everything the man wanted to know, and wasn't terrified. Her contempt for the man was overwhelming: she would never lower herself to be afraid of a piece of dirt like him.

Or rather, she tried to scream, but before she could scream she found her mouth filled with cotton wool, then the photographer forced her to sit down and held her firmly to the chair from behind.

'You still have time to tell the truth.' The man had sat down on her knees to stop her from kicking. At last she understood what that short-sighted look meant: he was a sadist, in the most technical sense of the word. 'I could hit you and knock you out, then while you're out I could slash your wrists. That would be amusing for the police: Oh look, we keep finding women with their wrists slashed, what on earth does it mean?' His voice had become soft and unctuous, but it didn't scare her, only disgusted her. 'But I need you alive, I need you to talk. I'm telling you for the last time, if you want to tell me the truth I'll take the cotton wool out.'

She shrugged, and told him with her eyes that he was mad, that she had told him everything she knew.

'Then I'll start with an incision on your forehead, I'm generous and I'll do it high up, that way you'll easily be able to hide it with your hair.' He rubbed her forehead with the alcohol, like an attentive nurse. 'I don't want to hurt you, I only want to disfigure you, at least if you don't talk.'

She almost didn't feel the cut, nor did any blood run down her face, because he scrupulously dabbed the wound with the peroxide while the photographer left her head free for a moment.

'If you have anything new to tell me, nod your head and I'll take out the cotton wool, but if you're going to tell me again that you don't know anything, then forget it, I'll only get angry.'

Maybe that noise was only in her mind, an auditory hallucination which she heard because of her hope that the noise was real, but she instinctively turned her head towards the door because she had heard the sound of the bell.

'Did someone just ring?' the man asked.

'No,' the photographer said. 'She must be waiting for somebody, and she thought they rang.'

The man reflected, with the penknife in his hand, so close to her face that she could see it was a promotional object and read on the handle the name of a famous brand of liqueurs. 'If she was expecting someone, they'd be here by now, so try to keep calm. This girl knows where the film from last year is, maybe she even has it, and she'll tell us eventually.' He rubbed her left cheek with the alcohol. 'If you talk,' he said to her, 'you'll avoid a cut on your cheek which no amount of plastic surgery will put right.' He looked at her and waited, then made the incision, his eyes almost closed behind his glasses, staring at her cheek like a diligent schoolboy at the page of an exercise book on which he's carefully writing a beautiful sentence. 'Whatever you know, you can't use it against us anyway. Tell your friends, if you have any, but if you talk I'll stop here.' He started dabbing the cut with the peroxide, but it wasn't enough, rivulets of blood started falling onto her neck, her chest, all the way to her stomach. 'Will you talk or shall I continue?'

4

First they saw Livia's taxi pull up. Even without the little telescope he had a good view of his Livia getting out in front of the stark, imposing temple of construction, but he used the telescope anyway to look at her more closely. He very much liked the dark red cotton dress she was wearing, she had good taste in clothes, her simplicity was so calculated, it was almost irritating. Then Livia was swallowed up by that deity of concrete and the taxi driver angrily headed back towards the heedless, sleeping metropolis. It was a few minutes after two, her punctuality was also irritating.

Their observation point was under the arbour, which rested against the roof of a tiny ramshackle house, like those you found in magazines for little children. Around the house and the arbour there were trees with bright, tiny leaves that created an ideal barrier, because from the outside you couldn't see anything and from inside you could see everything. Inside the house there was a fat young man sleeping with his head propped on the table. They had given him five thousand lire and this had relaxed him completely and had removed any curiosity he might have had. There was a side road, about a hundred metres long, joining the little house to the main road, the Giulietta was parked with its front towards the main road, in the shelter of the trees, and they were leaning on the trunk of the Giulietta in the relatively cool shade, watching.

'Has she gone in?' Davide asked.

'Yes.' Duca handed him the telescope. But now there was

nothing to be seen except the sky-grey tower in the green sea of fields and, in the background, Milan in the summer haze. It would have made a nice picture postcard, photographed from here, they could have offered it to the owners of the Ulisse Apartments.

A lorry passed, a moped passed, then nothing: the desert. Then Davide said, 'I think someone is about to stop outside the building.'

'What?' But he had already seen it: a Mercedes 230 had appeared from the end of the street and was now slowing down in front of the building then entering the scorching concrete parking area and very slowly parking between the white lines.

Davide was still looking through the telescope. 'I've seen that car before, the same model, the same colour, it must be the same, there aren't many Mercedes 230s around and it's unusual for two of them to have the same colour.'

'Where did you see it?' Now a man was slowly getting out, he looked young, though rather large, and seemed to be in absolutely no hurry.

Davide's voice was anxious. 'Last year, that day with Alberta.'

'Give me the telescope.' He looked through it at the young man, and saw him as if he was only about five metres away. To many he might have seemed the model of the good son, but to Duca, a doctor and psychologist despite every-thing, he didn't. That was the worst kind of criminal face there was, the kind that didn't arouse suspicion.

'On the autostrada, I saw it a couple of times before we

got to Somaglia, then when I came back towards Milan and Alberta was crying, it was still behind us. At Metanopoli I overtook it and it seemed as if it was going to stop.' Even after a year, the memory was still vivid, everything connected with Alberta was vivid in his mind. He now realised what that car had meant, a year earlier, and what it meant now.

Duca, too, had understood. 'He really looks like a killer,' he said, putting the telescope down on the trunk of the Giulietta. There was nothing else to see, the killer had entered the building, the Mercedes was baking in the sun.

'What should we do?' Davide asked, he seemed to have turned green, but it wasn't because of the reflection of the leaves in the arbour.

There was almost nothing they could do. Everything was clear. The distinguished-looking gentleman with the grey moustache seduced restless girls from the city, someone professional photographed them, and this man in the Mercedes kept an eye on them and punished those who rebelled or tried to get away or had the idea of betraying them. In addition, the photographs were hot. For a photograph, these people were prepared to kill one, two, ten women.

'We have to go in there now,' Davide said.

Yes, of course, they had to get going immediately: the man who had overpowered Alberta and slashed her wrists, who had taken Maurilia to Rome and drowned her in the Tiber, would also kill Livia Ussaro at the slightest suspicion.

'We have to stay here,' Duca said. He had the feeling he was also becoming green, at least the skin of his face felt as if it must be green.

'But that's the man who killed Alberta, he was following us the whole time.'

'Yes, that's him. But if we go in now, once we've knocked down the front door of the building and then the door of the apartment, he can kill Livia if he wants to, he has all the time in the world.' It was a simple and unfortunate situation, he explained, the only hope was that the man didn't suspect Livia, that he allowed her to pose for the photographs and then let her go, one of the many girls who must have passed that way. And there was no reason for him to suspect her: Livia hadn't met anyone after seeing Signor A, she had done nothing suspicious, she had left home and had come here to pose for photographs. Livia was clever, she knew what to do. Besides, if these people had had the slightest suspicion, they wouldn't even have got this far and stepped into a trap, they would have simply disappeared. They were on the lookout, but they didn't suspect. If they went up there to save Livia, they would simply kill her, because they would be revealing who she was. The best way to save her was to stay here, and wait for her to come out.

'And what if she doesn't come out?'

Young Davide's anxiety was making him nervous, he at least was hiding his own. 'They can't stay in there forever. Either they don't suspect anything, they photograph her and then let her go, or else they discover something and they'll try to escape.'

'And Livia?'

Enough now, he was also thinking of Livia, or maybe he was praying, rather than thinking. He didn't reply.

There are sixty minutes in an hour and they were passing one by one. The young man asleep in the little house from the kids' magazine woke up at the sound of a tractor passing on the main road, looked at the world outside, the Giulietta and the two men who were part of that world, then must have remembered the five thousand lire and lit a cigarette and probably started to think about the way he would spend it. It was no later than 2:25, it was just a matter of knowing how long it took a photographer to expose a complete roll of Minox film. He had no idea, it depended partly on the model, but he assumed it couldn't be less than half an hour.

Davide knew he shouldn't speak, but there was a limit. 'We can't just stay here and wait.'

'No,' Duca said, looking at his watch, almost exactly half an hour had passed since Livia had got out of the taxi. 'No, that's exactly what we have to do.'

And then something happened. They saw two men come out of the Ulisse Apartments and one of the two was the man from the Mercedes, who now seemed to be in a bit of a hurry, he was nowhere near as relaxed as he had been before, and, for not more than a thousandth of a second, they waited to see Livia, too, come out of that Aztec temple, but the two men were alone and had almost reached the Mercedes, and it really looked as if they were making a quick getaway.

'Try to cut them off,' he said to Davide. They had the disadvantage that they were nearly three hundred metres from the building, but the advantage that their car was ready, with its doors open, and they didn't have to do anything but start the engine. The other men were only now opening the doors of their car.

And in the time that took them, Davide set off, ate up the path, swallowed the two hundred metres of main road that separated them and aimed straight at the front of the Mercedes, practically determined to crash into it.

The Mercedes set off furiously: the road to Milan was near, and there they'd be able to lose themselves in the traffic. They rushed onto the main road towards Melzo, while Davide lost a few seconds reversing in order to point the car in the right direction. The man at the wheel of the Mercedes seemed to be very confident of the almost empty road, he still had three hundred metres advantage, he was moving straight ahead like a plane, and Duca then said something stupid to Davide: 'Even if we don't catch them, don't worry, we'll catch them later.'

'I've already got them,' Davide said. He was more than confident, he was blind with fury; as if the car ahead of them was a moped, he was suddenly on top of it, another second and he would overtake it.

'Watch out, they may turn off,' Duca said. He should also have said, watch out, they may open fire, but he didn't: if they opened fire they wouldn't be able to do anything about it.

The Mercedes did turn off, in fact, in order to avoid being boxed in on the main road, they must be intending to jump out and set off at a run across the fields, and if they did that it meant they weren't armed, and if they weren't armed they were dead, because the road they had been forced to turn onto was a mere hundred metres long and ended up in front of a big farmhouse.

Hens flew up into the air, a dog tied to a long chain howled and tried to fly, too, a countrywoman in shorts, bra, and straw hat stood there petrified with a kind of pitchfork in her hand when she saw the two cars explode in front of her, and they really did explode rather than just brake. The four doors of the two cars opened simultaneously, but Duca and Davide were faster on their feet, Duca grabbed the man, the sadist, before he had taken more than a few steps and before he realised that he had been caught, he gave him a kick in the stomach which laid him out flat in the dust in front of the farmhouse, howling and abject.

Davide had taken the other man and was holding him by one arm, without doing anything to him, because he was good, but the photographer was screaming hysterically, 'Help, help!' and it wasn't as stupid as it might seem to cry for help: if he managed to create confusion, if he could make the people here believe, if only for a minute, that he was an honest citizen being attacked, he might be able to get away.

Then Duca left the sadist moaning on the ground, unable to get up—if he hadn't smashed his stomach in it was pure chance, because that had been his intention—and passed on to the other man: he didn't yet know that he was a homosexual, but the way he was screaming aroused his suspicions and when he saw him up close his suspicions were confirmed.

'Look down, you bastard,' he said.

This unexpected request made the photographer fall silent for a moment, then he raised his head a little more and screamed even more loudly, 'Help!' That was all Duca needed: he hit him on his Adam's apple. Not even as a doctor had he ever been curious to know what happened to an Adam's apple if you hit it like that, for a moment all that happened was that the photographer fell abruptly silent and collapsed against Davide.

'Police,' Duca said.

A robust old countryman had suddenly appeared. Duca flashed his medical registration card at him: he was a romantic, he still kept it in his wallet.

'These two are murderers, they've killed two women, is there anywhere we can keep them locked up?'

Then a young man came out, then an old lady, then two boys. They weren't quite sure what was going on, but they all recognised the word 'police.'

'The stable,' the old man said.

'The stable will be fine.'

There was only an old carthorse there, it really was a stable, not one of those gleaming air-conditioned hostels you saw on television. They threw the two men down in the mire, one of them was moaning with his hands on his stomach, conscious but powerless to do anything, the other had fainted, or had he choked to death? Duca didn't think it was urgent to find out.

'Davide, go back to the Ulisse Apartments, find Livia, see what's happening, then phone Carrua, tell him everything and ask him to come here immediately.' This was urgent, Livia was urgent. 'In the meantime I'll talk to these two. Go.'

It isn't all that hot in a stable, in summer the smell is

stronger than the heat. The light came from two round holes high in the walls, but it was sufficient. Once he had heard Davide drive off, he forbade himself to think about anything apart from the two men. He stood in front of the one who was holding his hands on his stomach and had stopped moaning: his fear was greater than his pain.

'What did you do to the girl?'

'What girl?' He tried to pull himself up, because he could feel that muck which covered the floor of the stable like a Persian carpet seeping through his shirt.

With his foot, but without kicking him, only pressing, Duca forced him to lie down again in the mire. 'Listen to me,' he said, 'and I'm pleased to see that you've woken up, too,' he said to the other man who had opened his eyes and was gasping, 'that way you'll both hear my proposition. I ask questions and you answer. If your answers are the right ones, you'll just go to prison. If they're wrong, you'll go to the cemetery, I'll pull you to pieces, bit by bit, bone by bone, the police will have to call an ambulance with a waterproof tarpaulin. Do we agree? Just now, I asked you what you did to the girl. You answered, what girl? That's not the right answer. Now I'll ask you again, and try to answer correctly, it'll be in your best interests: What did you do to the girl?'

Silence. The horse didn't even turn its head, it seemed to be made of wood.

'I realised she'd been sent there by the police, I had my suspicions, so I had to make her talk.'

'What did you do to her?'

The sadist retched a bit, his body contorted by the pain

in his stomach, then he told Duca what he had done to her. And Duca did nothing, he stood there motionless, trying not to think about Livia.

'And did she talk?' he asked.

No, the sadist replied, she had continued to take those cuts on her face and continued to make it clear to him that she had nothing to say, and after a while he had almost been convinced that she hadn't come there to spy on him, so he had let her go and they had left.

'Why didn't you kill her? She has a lot to say now.'

'I'm not a murderer.'

'That isn't the right answer.' He kicked him hard with the heel of his shoe, almost on the temple, where it joined the jaw. He heard a groan, but the man didn't lose consciousness, which was just the way Duca wanted it: he would tear him apart, pull him to pieces, but wouldn't knock him out. 'You *are* a murderer, and if you didn't kill her you must have had your reasons. It'll be better for you if you tell me.' The man thought he was being clever, he closed his eyes and pretended he had fainted, he didn't know he was out of luck: his interrogator was a doctor. 'You can't fool me, I know you haven't fainted. Answer, or I'll continue.'

The man immediately opened his eyes again. 'They told me to do it, it's not up to me, I have to do what they tell me.'

'Yes, I know what they told you. Sometimes you kill and sometimes you scar. It's an old system. You're not in the Mafia, but you've been trained by Mafiosi, you must have taken a crash course in how to scar someone's face. Or am I wrong?'

The man said nothing.

'Answer me.'

He looked at the heel of the shoe one centimetre from his nose. 'In Turin I met two men from the south, but I was young, I did it almost as a game.'

'Of course, they taught you the anatomy of the facial muscles, the place to make the incision and the type of incision to make, an M-shaped incision, for example, can't be mended with plastic surgery.' These were things his father had explained to him, when he had started wearing long trousers and his father had finally been able to talk to him about the Mafia. He wouldn't have devoted a single minute to this whole business if he hadn't sensed the ruthless, violent hand of the Mafia behind it. No, these two louts weren't in the Mafia, nor was their local boss, or even their national boss, probably, but the theoretician, the mastermind of the whole system was certainly in the Mafia and took fifty per cent.

'Leaving a woman who's been scarred like that in circulation is good publicity, almost better than a woman who's been murdered. The papers talk about it, the girls get scared, if they don't behave the same thing will happen to them. When you have hundreds and hundreds of women who know a lot, and who'd like to go back to their previous lives, it isn't easy keeping them in their place, but with the methods your instructors from the Mafia have taught you, you can deal with them. And now tell me about the man with the grey moustache who picked up the girl last night. Who is he?'

No answer.

'Look, I know a lot, I know there are three of you, that man who's the local boss, you and your friend here. You only know your boss, but he must know a lot of interesting people. Give me his name and address. You're not a real Mafioso, the two of you are just pupils, you won't be able to hold out.' Delicately he placed his foot on the man's stomach and started to press.

The man screamed that he'd had enough, he retched, then gave Duca the name and address, and some other things, too, some very interesting things.

'Good, now if you want to keep your stomach, tell me, in detail, how you killed Alberta Radelli.'

With Duca's foot on his stomach, the man told him immediately. He had understood. Duca listened to him, and as he listened he realised that his father had been right. 'You have to speak their language. You can't speak French to someone who only understands German.' Of course it wasn't right, of course a police force that acts correctly doesn't use the language of violence, there are fingerprints, laboratory tests, well-conducted interrogations, psychological persuasion. But he wasn't the police, he was a young loser who couldn't hear the word Mafia without seeing his father with his arm stunted by a stab wound and reduced for ever, by that stab wound, to being a grey clerk in the Headquarters building, second floor, room 92, right at the back. Yes, he knew, it was just a common, ancestral thirst for revenge: he hadn't been looking for justice, he hadn't been trying to uphold the law, he had only wanted to see some of them face to face, and speak their language to them because that way you understood each other immediately.

'And now tell me how you killed Maurilia. In case you've forgotten, that's the blonde girl you took to Rome.'

No, no, he remembered perfectly well, because the more he remembered the less Duca's heel sank into his stomach, and he told the story with so many details it was almost like a novel. And then everything was clear, in every detail, and he was about to lift his foot from that stomach when the other man, the photographer, who had been so still on his bed of manure, had the bright idea of grabbing his leg. In his warped mind, it had occurred to him that Duca was there, his feet within reach of his hands, but he hadn't thought it out. Duca, though, had already thought of it and was perfectly calm, he had one hand resting on the horse's mane, and as soon as the photographer had grabbed his foot, he held on tight to the horse and with the same foot that the man was holding, kicked him in the face, twice, three times, until the man let go of his foot, moaning, and then he kicked him again, even harder, and the moaning immediately stopped.

The other man was sheltering his face with his hands. 'No, no, no,' he was saying.

But he had to be kept quiet, too, otherwise he might try to escape and that wasn't good. 'No, no, don't worry.' He didn't even kick him so hard, just enough to knock him unconscious for a while. Then he left the stable and lit a cigarette.

They arrived two minutes later. Davide in front in the Giulietta, followed by Carrua in the police Alfa Romeo, then the van for transporting prisoners.

'I told you not to get mixed up in this,' Carrua screamed as he got out, very angry, as if it weren't just a formality: he had known everything about the investigation from the start, through Mascaranti.

'They're in the stable,' Duca said. 'I can come over tonight and give you a report, they've already told me a lot of things. Be careful, there's a horse in the stable, it's very nervous, it keeps kicking, it must have kicked those fellows a few times.'

Carrua turned red. 'If you laid one finger on them I'll put you inside. Where are you going?'

He didn't reply, he'd stopped listening to Carrua's yelling. He took Davide by the arm and led him towards the Giulietta. 'Take me straight to the centre of town.' He didn't ask him anything until they were near the Via Porpora, queuing like robot sheep in the traffic that had resumed in all its fury. Then all he said was: 'Did you see her?'

He nodded, yes, he had seen her. That meant that he had gone to the Ulisse Apartments, rushed up to the second floor and seen Livia Ussaro.

'Was she conscious?'

'Yes.'

That meant that she hadn't fainted, that she was sitting on a chair, naked, with all the chess pieces lying on the floor around her, and she was dabbing her face with a towel, there wasn't much blood, no, there really wasn't much blood, but she had been about to faint when he had seen her face, when she had lowered the towel for a moment to let herself be dressed, because he had had to dress her, but she didn't faint, she hadn't fainted once, not even when he had taken her down to the car, she had even tried to walk by herself, barely supported.

'Where did you take her?'

'To the Fatebenefratelli Hospital, Carrua told me to do that on the telephone.'

'Let's go there now.'

'We can't.'

Then Duca noticed that Davide's body was moving convulsively, like children who have cried too much, at first it seemed like a kind of sobbing, but then he understood. And he also understood why they couldn't see her: she was being put back together. The worst thing, apart from the scars, was the vertical cuts at the corners of her lips—his father had once described to him in detail a full facial scarring—that would make it difficult for her to speak or eat for several weeks. Until she had been mended a little, they wouldn't be able to see her.

'Then let's go straight to the Piazza Castello.' He told Davide where they were going, who they were going to see, and what they were going to do, and how he, Davide, could help him. 'Let's hope he doesn't get out the back way,' he said.

They left the car in the Piazza Castello and went the rest of the way on foot. After a while they reached the characteristically narrow old lane, where there was a shop for stamp collectors that seemed out of place here, with two pocket-sized windows on either side of the entrance displaying lots of beautiful stamps that probably nobody had ever looked at, not even the owner. They went in and walked down two steps into a little room, not much larger than a toilet, which functioned, with a certain claim to elegance, as the kingdom of philately.

There was nobody there, and it was very dark. Display cases hanging on the wall, stuffed full of stamps, gleamed dimly. Lying open on the counter was a very large album, then there was a small armchair, and a big red glass ashtray, which not only didn't have any cigarette ends in it but was also veiled with dust: Signor A must have followed his doctor's advice and stopped smoking some time ago. But above all there was silence, and when they had opened the door no bell had rung.

'Is there anybody here?' he asked politely, staring politely at the half-open door at the back, and then he understood the reason for the sense of unease he had been feeling: somebody he couldn't see was looking at him from one of those display cases hanging on the wall, one of the stamps wasn't a stamp, but a hole in the wall that you could look through from the other side. With really childish curiosity, he would have liked to know which stamp it was.

The little door at the back finally opened completely and an elegant gentleman appeared, smiling. He had a grey moustache, he was exactly as Livia had described him: Signor A.

'I'm so sorry . . .' Signor A's intention was to apologise for keeping them waiting, but from across the counter the two of them grabbed him, dragged him over the counter and wedged him into the armchair, and Duca stunned him with a slap while Davide searched him.

'Yes, here it is.'

It was a woman's revolver: Signor A probably didn't always carry it, he must have stuffed it in his pocket when he heard them come in.

'Look for the light switch,' he said to Davide, 'then lower the shutter, go in the back, block the door and phone Carrua, tell him he can come and get another one.'

The slap—although the word wasn't entirely accurate, more like an understatement—had turned one of Signor A's eyes red with blood, but he hadn't emitted a moan or said a word.

Duca now said something very specific. 'Your friend the photographer and the other man have already told me a lot,' he said. 'Now it's your turn to tell me all you know. There must be little shops like this in other cities in Italy, and you must also be in contact with people abroad. I need names, addresses, and details. Davide, find some paper and come here and write,' he said to Davide, then turned back to the silent Signor A, who was not only silent but had the stony look on his face of someone who would never talk. 'You're over fifty, I give you my word as a doctor that you won't be able to stand more than three blows to the liver, at the third everything will burst inside you. This is number one.'

At the same time, he covered the man's mouth with his hand, but Signor A did not even have the strength to moan, his eyes looked as if they were coming out of their sockets, they lost that stony *I'll never talk* look, and Duca asked him the first question.

'Please answer at once.'

Breathing heavily, his nose now as white as his lips, he answered. Then he answered the second question, and the third, and the fourth, he answered all the questions.

'Names and addresses.'

He gave names and addresses, but was starting to moan and to bend double.

'Tell me everything, or I'll hit you again.' He might not survive even a second blow, whatever the doctors did to save his liver, but Duca would hit him all the same, and Signor A understood that and gave him the last name, the last address, the one he had promised over and over again never to reveal.

'Yes, I think you've told me everything.' He looked at him and thanked him. 'Thank you, you've been very good.'

Davide had covered almost three large sheets of paper. Then they pulled up the shutter, switched off the light, and waited in the gloom, while the little boss moaned. They would get the big guys soon enough.

Then Mascaranti arrived with two officers and took away Signor A and the three written sheets, and Duca and Davide were free.

5

'It's over,' Duca said to Davide.

They walked back to the Giulietta. It was all over, all had been explained, it was so nastily simple. 'Let's go back to the Cavour, at least to pay the bill.'

From the furnace of the streets they entered the spring-like mountain air of the Cavour. They asked for the bill and two bottles of beer. In the room, he took off his jacket, but didn't invite Davide to take off his, because he always kept it on. He sat down on the bed and phoned the Fatebenefratelli Hospital. The switchboard operator put him through to the ward, the ward sister told him to wait, then he heard his colleague's voice.

'Lamberti here.'

Hearty greetings from his colleague: he was a veteran, with a protective tone.

'Nearly two hours ago they brought in a girl with her face cut up.'

Yes, his colleague said, replying to his questions, they had just finished dressing her wounds, no, she wasn't in a state of shock, no, her general condition was fine, and she was in good spirits, she was an incredible girl, he said, she had tried to smile, and then he told him all the technical details of the scars, which was what he really wanted to know.

'I'll be over to see her in an hour, will you still be there?'

Yes, his colleague would still be there and would be happy to see him. Good. 'I've finished with you too, Davide,' he said, putting down the receiver. 'You don't need me any more.' He wouldn't drink again, even though he would never be a teetotaller. Davide said nothing.

'Listen, I need two favours,' he said at the front door of the hotel. 'Firstly, can you be my driver for another couple of errands?'

Davide nodded.

'Secondly, if your father's in Milan, I need to see him as soon as possible.'

Davide nodded.

'Now take me to the Via Plinio.' He also nodded. 'That's right, to Livia's apartment.'

Davide drove slowly. 'How is Livia?'

'They told me she's fine.' It wasn't much of an answer, but there wasn't much to say.

In the Via Plinio he got out. 'Wait for me,' he told Davide. He went in through the front door and came out nearly half an hour later. 'Let's go to the Fatebenefratelli.' Then it really would be over. When Davide stopped the car outside the hospital, he put a hand on his arm. 'Don't come in to see Livia, you've already seen her enough.'

Duca went into the hospital. A male nurse recognised him and greeted him impulsively, saying he was really pleased to see him. He got to the ward and met the colleague he had spoken to on the phone, who was about to leave and wasn't wearing his white coat. The veteran embraced him, he was discreet and sensible, he didn't ask any questions, just replied to Duca's, which were technical, purely technical, and then he took him to Livia's room.

'Bye for now, anything you need, I'm here,' his colleague said.

'Thanks,' he said. He closed the door behind him and looked at the screen, beyond the screen was the bed with Livia in it. Before going around the screen he said, 'It's me, Livia.'

He went around the screen and stopped for a moment at the foot of the bed, looking at her. Then he moved a chair close to her and sat down. 'First of all, I wanted to say one thing: I've just been to see your father. I told him you've been given a very confidential task by the police and will be away for a while. He was surprised, of course, but I managed to convince him, though I'll get Mascaranti to talk to him, too, I'm sure he can convince him better than I could. You mustn't worry about your family.'

To stop her moving her eyelids, because of the cuts at the corners, they had bandaged her eyes, which was why Livia Ussaro—it wasn't in any way a pseudonym, it was the name of a real, aching, wounded but undefeated human being— lifted her hand, which lay on top of the sheet, and searched for his hand, which she found immediately and squeezed a little, once, twice: it was her way of saying thank you, given that she could not speak. It was clear that, for her, there was nothing personal, let alone affectionate, in that touch of hands, it was just a means of communication, a way of telling him that she was listening and understood what he was saying.

'They've all been arrested, all the ones from here in Milan,' he said. To any other woman, he might have said something else, hoped that she would get better soon, told her that these days plastic surgery can do wonders, that in a few weeks . . . and so on and so forth, but not to Livia Ussaro: she was either thinking and hoping these things for herself and didn't need anyone to tell her, or else she wasn't thinking or hoping them and if anyone had told her she would have been annoyed. 'We have the names of lots of other bosses, from all over Europe. Now Interpol will get to work. They were organised and taught by the Mafia to do a top-class job for a top-class clientele. Every woman was selected among the thousands of likely ones in a big city. Even prostitution has been declining for years, above all, so Signor A told me, because of the low quality of the merchandise. Under the guidance of the Mafia, a few big wheels on the business decided to set up a deluxe prostitution ring. The same women, once exploited in this way, could then be moved into the lower categories . . . Am I tiring you?' It was a pointless scruple that had occurred to him abruptly—after all, a few hours earlier Livia had been at the mercy of a sadist—but the pressure of Livia's hand on his told him that he had made a blunder. He had to continue: the best cure for Livia was for him to talk.

'The search for this select merchandise was the most delicate part of the operation. They weren't dealing with corrupted young girls any more, who were easy to persuade and to keep in line with a few slaps. They had to find new girls, or almost new, like Alberta, girls from decent families who agreed to it at first and then regretted it after they'd learned too much about the organisation and sometimes rebelled.

If they hadn't been harsh with them, the business wouldn't have lasted more than a few weeks, that was why every group had a man like the one you met today.'

The young man made the reluctant ones think again and punished the rebels. Apart from that, he had the task of taking the girls to their various places of employment.

'The Minox photographs had two purposes,' he continued, looking everywhere as he talked except at the white bandages concealing her face. 'One was to compile a kind of catalogue of rare editions, so to speak, which circulated all over Europe, constantly updated, among connoisseurs and people in the trade. The other was to blackmail the women who had been photographed. Most of the reluctant ones yielded when they were threatened with the photographs being shown to their fathers, their boyfriends, their workmates. With Alberta it was different, she did more than just rebel, she actually took the Minox film after it was exposed.'

That had been serious, he told her, continuing to keep his hand open on the bed, with her hand on his, ready to press his fingers, to respond, to ask. It had probably never happened before that anyone had stolen a roll of film. The whole elegance of the mechanism was based on the secrecy of those films, and in order to maintain that secrecy photographic studios that seemed above board had been set up in the cities. The photographer shot models of cars, tractors, and tankers for serious companies against a landscape background, publicity photographs and industrial photographs that wouldn't arouse the suspicion of the police. Doing the photographs in a private house might have been dangerous, with different girls coming and going constantly, they needed a name plate with Something-or-other Photographic written on it, and in fact the system had been functioning perfectly for nearly two years all over Europe on this side of the curtain, because on the other side they were organised differently, and now here was Alberta taking that Minox cartridge, risking the whole system crashing down because even the most stolid of police officers would realise what a roll of film like that was as soon as he saw it.

'That was when the man you met today went into action. He couldn't scare Alberta and she managed to get away, so he got hold of the other girl, Maurilia, and threatened to kill her if Alberta didn't hand over the cartridge.' It was quite dark in the room, even darker now because the sun, even though it was not setting yet, had become only a dusty source of heat more than of light, but it was a merciful darkness because this way even though he was looking at the bed, the deep shadows were hiding the details of her bandaged face and gradually even the very shape of her face.

Alberta had then realised—he explained lucidly, without anything anxious in his voice—that even if she handed over the cartridge, they would kill her poor friend and then her, and in fact she was right, because Maurilia had already been taken to Rome and drowned and they were only waiting for the moment to get her, too.

Alberta had had a shock, suddenly she realised what a pit of vice and violence she had fallen into. She was an inflexible woman, even with herself: she would hand over the cartridge to the police and tell them everything, then kill herself. That was why she had that letter for her sister in her handbag. Before killing herself, though, she had to get her sister the fifty thousand lire to pay the expenses on her rented apartment—she was inflexible even in small things—and she got it for her in the only way she could at that moment, by looking for a man. And she found Davide.

She knew she was being followed and was in danger, but she still mingled with people and when Davide agreed to give her a lift she felt safer. But then Davide's company brought on a crisis in her, she felt weak, she wanted to live, it struck her that if she could get away, a long way away, things would be different, but Davide had no idea of the reasons for this crisis and at the end of the autostrada he had made her get out. And that man was there, in his Mercedes 230.

'You can imagine what happened. The man asked her for the cartridge, but she'd left it in Davide's car, she hadn't even realised and had no idea why she didn't have it. He didn't believe her, he searched in her handbag, found the letter addressed to her sister, the devil was offering him the perfect opportunity. He overpowered her, made his incisions, and left her in that field.' He was a practical man when it came to using a knife. 'And he also took forty thousand of the fifty thousand lire that Davide had given Alberta, he's not the kind of man who can look indifferently at a bunch of ten-thousand-lire notes.' Even though the police were still investigating those two not very convincing suicides, they wouldn't get anywhere without the Minox film. But the cartridge, together with a little handkerchief once soaked in tears, had been in Davide's suitcase for a whole year as he descended into psychosis and alcoholism.

Now he had to continue speaking because with every pause he made she pressed with her fingers on the palm of his hand. And luckily it was almost impossible to see anything now, and luckily again the nurse came in and said, 'Are you Dr. Lamberti?'

He said yes, he was, although it was a heavy burden being Duca Lamberti at that moment.

'There are two people here who want to speak to you.'

He squeezed Livia's hand. 'I'll only be gone a moment, Livia, I'll be right back.' She pressed his palm, to tell him he could go.

In the corridor stood Davide and his father, still little, still an emperor, still supremely self-confident.

'I'm sorry Davide made you come here, it wasn't so urgent.'

'Don't bother to stand on ceremony, Davide told me you wanted to see me immediately.'

All right, Caesar, don't get angry. 'Before anything I wanted to hand your son back to you.' A nun passing in the corridor recognised Duca and smiled. 'He's never been an alcoholic and will never be one. And he's not a big lump either, as you told me.'

The little man looked at Davide. 'I hope the doctor's diagnosis is correct.'

'Completely correct. Also, I need a favour.' He asked him if, in a few weeks' time, he could bring a girl who had been disfigured in an accident to his villa near Inverigo, where she would be able to stay in seclusion until she was a little better.

'Davide told me it wasn't a car accident,' Caesar said, with dismay. 'Horrendous. I'll do everything I can to help you and the girl. The villa is at your disposal as of now.'

'Thank you.'

'Can I come in, just for a moment?' Davide ventured.

His tone was imploring, but Duca shook his head, it was better not. 'Maybe tomorrow. But now you can do me a favour, too. Go and see my sister, she hasn't heard from me in a while. Tell her a few things, and if you don't have any other commitments, keep her company.' Lorenza lived alone too much, he had to sort things out for her in some way. He also had to sort things out for himself.

He said goodbye to the two Auseris, went back into the room, and said, 'It's me.' He sat down next to the bed, put his hand on the bed with the palm open, next to hers, and she immediately put her fingers on it and pressed. She wanted him to talk. His brain was seething, but he had to find something that Little Miss General Topics would like. Euthanasia, there it was, he had never talked to her about it, and yet she was an admirer of his, this was the moment to make her happy.

'Three years ago, when I was sentenced . . .' he began. He would explain the whole theory of euthanasia, and she would be happy, even in that hospital room, even disfigured and bandaged, because there were things in life that mattered more to her than the scars, there was thought with a capital T, there were theories, there was justice, and so on . . . 'The thing about euthanasia . . .' and he squeezed her fingers tenderly.

Translator's notes

Montecatini: a major Italian chemicals company.

Princess Soraya: former wife of the Shah of Iran, who had a brief European film career in the 1960s.

Françoise Hardy: French pop singer, at the height of her fame in the 1960s.

Salò: Fascist republic set up by Mussolini in northern Italy in 1943 after the Allied landings in the south.

Idroscalo: a park with a large artificial lake and a range of recreational facilities, near Linate Airport.

Milva: popular Italian singer and actress.

Montesi affair: scandal that erupted after the body of an aspiring actress named Wilma Montesi was found on a beach near Rome in 1953. Various members of Rome's high society were implicated in the subsequent investigations, but the murder was never solved.

Categorical imperative: one of the major concepts of the German philosopher Immanuel Kant. *Prolegomena to any future metaphysics that will be able to present itself as a science* is a work by Kant, published in 1783.

La Rinascente: chain of department stores, with branches in several major Italian cities.

Vilfredo Pareto: Italian sociologist, economist, and philosopher.

TRAITORS TO ALL

Winner of the Grand Prix de Littérature Policière

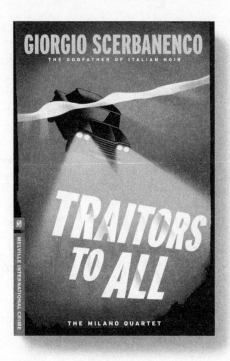

In the second book of the Milano Quartet, Duca Lamberti
investigates a crime whose roots go back to World War II,
and a shocking act of betrayal.

$16.95 U.S./Can.
Paperback: 978-1-61219-336-3
Ebook: 978-1-61219-367-0

Ⓜ MELVILLE INTERNATIONAL CRIME